The New York Diaries

Daniel Drennan

The New York Diaries

TOO-TRUE TALES OF URBAN TRAUMA

BALLANTINE BOOKS ● NEW YORK

A Ballantine Book
Published by The Ballantine Publishing Group

Copyright © 1998 by Daniel Drennan

http://www.randomhouse.com

Grateful acknowledgment is made to *The New York Times* for permission to reprint an excerpt from "No Fare, and No Handcuffs" by Clifford Krauss, December 6, 1995. Copyright © 1995 by The New York Times Company. Reprinted by permission.

Library of Congress Cataloging-in-Publication Data
Drennan, Daniel.
The New York diaries : too-true tales of urban trauma / Daniel Drennan. — 1st ed.
p.   cm.
ISBN 0-345-41643-0 (alk. paper)
1. New York (N.Y.)—Social life and customs—20th century—Humor.   2. City and town life—New York (State)—New York—Humor.   3. Drennan, Daniel—Homes and haunts—New York (State)—New York—Humor.   I. Title.
F128.55.D74   1998
974.7'1043—dc21   98-19282
CIP

Text design by Fritz Metsch

Manufactured in the United States of America

First Edition: September 1998

10   9   8   7   6   5   4   3   2   1

For Hervé

Contents

Why I Stay

I want to be a part of it: New York, New York. . . .
— "New York, New York," played at every single
high school dance I ever went to

My formative years were spent in the Levitt-created exurbia constructed in a formerly virgin New Jersey of farmland and forests, located equidistant between Philadelphia and New York City just outside of New Brunswick, a decidedly middle-class pre-fab insta-town tucked well outside the equestrian enclaves to the north and the tony Princetonian estates to the south. Most of the people resettling in New Jersey at the time were urban-weary New Yorkers like my father, tired of New York living and vowing not to raise their children in the City, a place communicated to us in stories as one where anything and everything could happen and did. Trips into the City to visit relatives were a fascinating glimpse into a lifestyle that wasn't mine: apartment living, crowded noisy streets, not much in the way of grass or trees.

Like me, my friends in high school came from ex–New York families, with our teenage focus thus remaining decidedly New York–centric: concerts were in New York, art was in New York, theater was in New York, worthwhile thrift shopping was in New York. Even though we lived an equal distance from Philadelphia, our cultural references were resolutely New York–based: New York metropolitan area television stations all numbered 13 or less, while strange Philadelphia-based stations buzzed somewhere off in the fuzzy UHF band with numbers like 29 and 48, good for *Night Gallery* reruns and not much more; our days of summer were spent with escapees from New York on the way to Seaside Heights, while Philly kids preferred Wildwood, two beach cultures worlds apart though both in the same small state. It was thus with equal parts filial rebellion and northern New Jersey chauvinism that I viewed New York as an exciting Mecca a meager forty miles from my house whose skyline was not readily visible on my horizon but whose endless lights made the cloudy night sky glow an off-yellow in the distance to the northeast.

Despite a detour to school in upstate New York and then in France, this dream of an electric and exciting

New York did eventually bring me here to live, and there are still times when I feel a sense of that New York–philia that brought me here in the first place, with New York Living at any given time being a unique balancing act between rapt upward-gazing naïve wonderment and downcast blinkered resolute fed-up-ness. People talk of the "excitement" and the "energy" and all of those other buzzwords that meaninglessly dot the pages of tourist brochures, all of those things New York is supposed to be, whereas I sometimes joke that the real reason I'm so at home in New York is that, with all my neuroses, New York City is the only place on Earth where I actually fit in. New York allows for honest and true individuality; the tics and quirks that anywhere else often need to be suppressed find glorious expression in the daily interaction of the City's inhabitants. The small adventure that has been my New York life is most obviously a story of change: neighborhood change, lifestyle change, habitude change; yet the basic rhythm stays the same, with people, places, and events coming and going like elements in a strange fugue, or in the chessboard life of Alice beyond her looking glass. It is this—the banal, singular rhythm of life in New York—that makes the City endlessly new and exciting for me, and it is out of that rhythm that these stories spring.

Schadenfreude

I arrive in New York City after three years of study in Paris, all legal means to extend my Francophile lifestyle exhausted despite my having acquired the language, a dog, and a boyfriend (not necessarily in that order). The familiar Brooklynese of an airport worker exhorting non-natives to form a line to the right in ever-louder levels of frustrated not-understood English is a pleasure to hear, yet is given a contextual twist later by the conversation I overhear between customs workers discussing the new requirement to learn a second language, when, after all, "This is America; *we talk English here*." Traveling with most of my former French life depressingly reduced to a few suitcases, I make an attempt to reassemble my earthly belongings (including my fuzzy-headed tranquilized dog) in order to speed my trip through customs. I carefully pile up my luggage on a cart and tether my scrawny bundle-of-black-fur dog to the front, all while holding his papers in one hand and my passport in my teeth, expecting a bit of a battle with the customs official—who to my great surprise waves me right through. The exit doors open automatically as I push my cart into the arrivals terminal with my waiting parents and other assorted expectant faces lined up on both sides; my drug-induced foggy dog meanders unsurefootedly in front of me, leaving me looking not unlike the Grinch arriving in Who-ville.

Unlike the Grinch, however, I have no Master Plan to accomplish in one single night, only vague ideas of eventually falling into a New York Groove. But a day-long frantic quest two weeks later looms as a sign of the times to come as I drive in circles around Newark Airport desperately unable to reach the customs building, which is tauntingly visible across the highway but which I can't actually *get to*, until I realize that the road sign I keep passing does not refer to an (in my mind) employees-only "service road" but to the proper-named *Service Road* that leads directly across the highway to my shipped body of work and trunks of art supplies.

I get reacquainted with the city by walking around

with my friend Laurel, and as we tour the army-navy stores, Canal Street, and other low-priced pre-Christmas thrift store–type shopping, on a whim we enter the Strand bookstore to see whether they are hiring, since I am not likely to be otherwise gainfully employed anytime soon. I fill out their application, which asks among other things for my ten favorite books—this request being perhaps the Strand's only pretension, since at the time it didn't have book readings, or a coffee bar, or author signings like the newfangled bookstore-slash-pickup-joints currently opening up around town—and my choices appear to pass muster since I am hired on the spot to start the next week, during the hectic Christmas shopping season, when the love/hate relationship that book buyers have with the Strand turns to pure hate, as employees recoil in the face of New Yorkers combing through the stacks of half-priced merchandise looking for anything remotely applicable present-wise for the subjacent regions of their holiday gift lists, and everyone's dispirited notion of the consumer basis of Christmas is pushed right over the edge into Pure Cynicism. The most difficult portion of my trial-by-fire training as a Strand cashier (other than getting breakfast for the entire store staff) involves learning how to divide the price of books in half without rounding the trailing ninety-five cents up into a full-dollar amount; this complex mathematical formula is of course not something that appears on SAT tests, or algebra quizzes, or intelligence tests of any kind, yet it is essential to achieving cashierhood at the Strand, and I don't quite understand why we can't just plug the exact amount into the cash register and hit a "half-price" key, since the register might be better equipped to take on the actual price calculation processes than we, the human cashiers.

The rest of my first day is passed safely behind the checkout counter watching the endless streams of people battling their way in and out of the store via one glass door trying to get past the determined individuals who are vocally protesting the veiled presumption of guilt that is the Bag Check, with one man's mounting anger resulting in a kicked-in front door; and as if being arrested for such ruckus-causing is not demeaning enough, his dignity is further insulted by a store manager who snaps a Polaroid, which later is added to the wall of personae non gratae mug shots behind the managers' counter. I stand there shocked; the other cashiers remain unfazed. Ten minutes later, another woman refuses to check her bag, protesting, "This is my *purse*! It is not my *bag*!" To which the irreverent manager notes dryly, "You could probably pack a ten-day vacation in that 'bag.'" The woman stands stock-still for a minute or so as a hush falls over the cashiers, starts changing colors as if she is holding her breath, and screams at the top of her lungs: "FUCKING SHIIIIIIIIIIIIT!" Then she turns around and calmly leaves the store. Someone applauds. This is only just my *first day*.

I quickly learn that as a Strand employee I am detested by great hordes of New Yorkers who are under the mistaken impression that the tens of thousands of books located in the "eight miles" of Strand bookshelves are somehow immediately findable by computer or organized by something resembling the Dewey Decimal System or otherwise memorized in workers' brains and that my response to their book-finding query—an attempt to explain that the bookstore is a chaotic anomaly in a world where people expect instantaneous information access and that shopping at the Strand involves actually *looking* for books, which in some former age was considered a *pleasure* of sorts—makes *me* somehow rude and obnoxious. Customers are upset that I can't lead them to a given book with any certainty, but, on the other hand, they don't appreciate my ability to name titles based on vague descriptions of past write-ups in *The New York Times Book Review* and half-correct author names, which in these days of immediate gratification and huge megastores is, I guess, a lost and definitely undervalued art.

Sometimes the employees snap in a big way, in a geyser-like overflow of pressure and vile epithets and obscene gestures, necessitating cooling-off periods downstairs, or managerial intervention. (I can't recall ever being reprimanded for yelling at a customer, the managers of the Strand knowing perhaps that if we were not allowed to fly off the handle from time to time we would *ourselves* come unglued—which is not to say that a lot of us were not halfway unglued *already*, but I think they preferred we be halfway unglued and fully employable as opposed to totally unglued and of use to absolutely no one.) Certain customers take the brunt of our otherwise-bubbling-beneath-the-surface jaded wrath: Carlos Castaneda fans who react in violent contrast to the teachings of their peaceful New Age guru when told to look in the fiction section, culty Aesthetic Realists with their "Victim of the Press" buttons who don't know quite what to make of our handmade "Victim of Aesthetic Realism" button rebuttals. Great fun is made of big-name authors buying their remaindered books or celebrities asking how to get downstairs while standing in front of the big directional DOWNSTAIRS sign. Certain rather adored customers receive affectionate nicknames, like the Cookbook Lady who saves her tips from her waitress job and then goes through stacks of cookbooks at closing time—at 9:29 she only starts *narrowing* her selection—and, when I ask her whether she is really going to cook all of this stuff, replies: "Oh, no! I just like to look at the pictures!" Or the Rosewater Lady smelling of Avon rose perfume who buys publishers' proofs and romantic paperbacks in scads and when I ask her where she keeps her books says: "Hell, honey, I've got books *behind my toilet*!"—which I have no reason to doubt whatsoever.

Unlike the night owl regulars for whom we stow titles from their favorite genres, or to whom we clandestinely explain how to stash books in unbrowsed shelves of the store for later retrieval, certain customers who bluster into the Strand have no bibliographic pretensions at

all—like the young couples decorating their first apartment who have no qualms about buying the expensive
leather-bound first editions behind the counter by the
shelf-full since they find books "wonderfully decorative,"
or the couple who drive up in a Rolls-Royce and immediately set to work buying up baskets of books, splitting up
to cover more territory, alternatingly and precipitantly
bringing up baskets of books, even though we are just-as-
quickly running out of room behind the registers for their
accumulating mountain of reading material, which, in
our pastime of psychoanalyzing people based on their
purchases, we notice is rather scattered in terms of subject matter. At one point the guy half of the book-buying
tag team asks us where the gal half is but walks away
before we have a chance to reply; later we tell the gal
half that "her husband" is looking for her. She hesitates,
realizes who it is we are referring to, and says: "That's
not my husband, *that's my interior decorator!*"

Plowing ahead, the woman says, "Where are the
purple books?" the same way someone might say "Where
is the fiction section?" or "Where is your medical reference?" We haltingly explain that the books are not actu-

ally organized by *color* so much as by *subject*, obviously greatly disappointing her in the process, as she delivers the coup de grâce that we, the bookstore workers who spend our paychecks on books like addicted laborers working in cocaine fields, dread to hear as we look to our great horror at the baskets piled up around our feet, the seeming randomness of their selections making sense as she responds: "Well, my decorator wants me to buy *only yellow and purple books!*"

Every day at the Strand ends with one of us cashiers seething and/or shaking and/or crying after the five-hundredth person calls us "freak" or "bitch" or informs us that "This ain't canned corn I'm buyin', sweetheart!"— which in and of themselves are tiny insignificant things but cumulatively take a toll, with post-work assuage-ment to be found at the Dugout, a little hole-in-the-wall around the corner as-of-then undiscovered by NYU frat boys where we daily decide that we will be quitting *very soon* to pursue Our Dreams Deferred, consisting of the usual gamut of artist/writer/actor ambitions and including my Great Plans of getting my art career off the ground, even though I continue to entertain my notions of a life in theater or film, belied by my meager résumé that consists of High School Drama Club, a rejection from NYU's drama school, a seen-only-from-the-back starring role in a student film at Syracuse University, and a beer commercial in Paris where my fifteen hours of work are condensed into one-eighth of one split second. Adding insult to psychological injury in terms of my specific thespian tragedy is the obstacle course I run of NYU film majors in Greenwich Village in the spring; compelled perhaps by cost and weight to not schlepp camera equipment all over town, they seem obliged to shoot their student films within a ten-block radius of their film school just down the street on Broadway. These are the student films they hope will make them famous and pay off their tens of thousands of dollars of debt but usually do neither, thus dooming them to their vengeful future as motion-picture-studio workers who regularly shut down entire city blocks at a time with their trailers, and klieg lights, and camera crews, and intern staffers who not-even-politely prevent people from walking down their own streets to get to their own places of residence, including people like me who secretly hope to be discovered, or used as an extra, or party to overheard gossip at the very least, but like me instead furrow their brows and haughtily demand passage to gain entrance to their *own buildings.*

After borderline suffocating all of one late spring day in the fan-blown age-old-book-dust-ridden un-air-conditioned Strand, I walk out of the store fairly exhausted with some of the other cashiers, no doubt Dugout-bound, when we notice one of our co-cashiers stretched out on the sidewalk with her head in the gutter. Being used to each other's strange quirks and daily outbursts, we do not find it so terribly out of the ordinary to see our co-worker this way, especially as it is much more bothersome to see great masses of New Yorkers strolling along on lower Broadway walking around and over her *without a second thought*; and further belying an emergency situation is the fact that our friend is lying there with her legs crossed and her hands folded across her stomach, as they might be if she were reclining on her couch in her living room, if, by chance, her couch were made out of *concrete.* Our initial reaction changes from slight shock to slight annoyance because of the way she is casually lying there, since, if you are going to block an entire New York City sidewalk with your own *body*, at the very least you probably shouldn't do it so *nonchalantly*.

"Hi," we say.

"Hi," she replies, squinting into the sun to look at us gathered around her.

Her insouciance is unsettling on some level, leaving us baffled as to what to say or do. I crouch down and sit on the curb to ask if she is okay; I try to prop her up, and I ask whether her immediate plans involve going home anytime soon, but she just wants to lie there some more; I try to coax her to at least get her head out of the gutter, since no matter what is really wrong it probably isn't a great idea to be so reposed on the hot pavement at 12th Street and Broadway, as if I would ever have to *convince* someone of that fact; and the other cashiers shrug their shoulders and look on, growing rather impatient with our in-the-gutter conversation.

Peripherally I perceive someone approaching rather determinedly, with some strange-looking camera apparatus in his hand; it could be some kind of weapon from the way he is zooming in on us, staring directly at us, not lifting his gaze from us not even for one second, until he is looming over us and I too am now squinting up to see who is there.

"Hi. I'm an NYU film student, and I'm making a student film for my thesis," he announces.

I stare, slightly dumbfounded, as he is joined by his friends, likewise laden with bulky film equipment, all equally oblivious to the fact that I am sitting on the curb having a conversation with someone lying prostrate on the sidewalk with her head in the gutter.

"I'm an NYU film student, and I'm making a student film for my thesis," he reiterates, "and I was wondering if you wouldn't perhaps want to be in it."

There should probably be a word in the English language, New Yorkese more specifically, equivalent to *schadenfreude*—satisfaction or pleasure felt at someone else's misfortune, like when you involuntarily yearn for the crash after hearing a skidding car slam on its brakes, or when you take special glee observing someone drop their double-shot latte on the way to work, or when you giddily watch the subway doors slam closed on the lummox levering entrance with his briefcase—only this new word would have the more extensive definition of "*personal selfish gain* derived at the *physical, emotional, or monetary expense* of someone else's misfortune," along the lines of *überschadenfreude*, perhaps. I look at the film student, and my friend in the gutter looks at me, evidently expecting to hear me say something along the lines of "Can't you see that my friend is troubled, lying in the street with her head in the gutter?"—and admittedly somewhere deep inside a voice is in fact angrily saying, "How can you possibly ask me that question when I am sitting here, trying to help my friend, sprawled on the filthy pavement with her head in the gutter?"—and I look up at him, and I look down at my friend, and I look up again as some *überschadenfreude* part of my being takes over and I say: "So . . . um, what kind of film is it, anyway?"

Real Estate

I was taking the M7 uptown bus the other day, and we were going through midtown and there were these two women seated in front of me; and in midtown there is this big clock which shows a readout of the national debt getting higher and higher, and this one woman is like, "Look, the national debt just gets higher and higher!" And I think to myself that maybe they should take the money that everyone saves with MCI—which is another *huge number readout sign in midtown—* and put that money toward paying off the national debt.

The search for a private space of one's own leads many New-Yorkers-to-Be to overlook certain inadequacies of city living: nonworking heat and plumbing, strangely sub-divided former tenements, raucous street noise. Since I am living with my parents while I work at the Strand, my personal workaday rhythm consists of a twice-daily mind-numbing commute to and from the Port Authority Bus Terminal, with its mocking plaster of Paris statue of wiped-out, stone-heavy, brain-dead passengers eternally approaching their frozen-in-time bus-gate Doors of Hell. Rushing commuters, dazed tourists, and out-of-it mar-ginal types all mix together, desperately wanting to go somewhere *else*, when they are not pushing or shoving or hungrily surrounding me hands outstretched panhan-dling at the Fanny Farmer candy counter as I order orange creams not for my own consumption but to satisfy my father's sweet tooth since he never seems to ask me how my day goes but rather whether I've brought home some *orange creams* for him. It is thus with overjoyed relief that I accept the offer of one of my co-Stranders to be the third roommate in her apartment on 13th Street between Third and Fourth Avenues, in which my niche of personal space is separated from hers by a sheet hanging where a door should be and is separated from my other roommate by his loft bed, under which I sleep at night, with the five-foot-eleven-inch width of the windowless room and the five-foot-eleven-inch height of the homemade loft bed forcing me at six-foot-one to crook my head to one side whenever I need to, say, *stand up* or *sleep*. Considering myself fortunate compared to the Port Authority bad dream I am leaving behind, I happily pile my books and clothes in milk crates and sleep on a futon on the floor and ignore both the apartment door that not only opens directly into but also bisects completely our one shared living space—which serves as foyer, dining room, and kitchen—and the appalled speechlessness of my father as he helps me move in.

Our neighbors—probably not the best word to

describe the people we share the building with since we are only vaguely made aware of their existence by the incomprehensible Spanish screaming next door, or the sight of indistinct nakedness behind half-closed window shades across the alleyway—are a mix of people our age squeezed into apartments like ours, remnant tenants from an earlier time, and relatively well-off newer tenants, reflecting our equally mixed neighborhood, which borders Greenwich Village to the west, New York University to the south, and the East Village, with the former bookstores and the schmatte trade of Broadway giving way to the dorms of NYU, high-priced antique dealers, and the clothing emporia that draw baggy-jeaned puffy-jacketed kids from all over the city to what is now of course Prime Real Estate Central. The only neighbor I ever address any words to is the man who lives directly upstairs, most often viewed dragging the filthiest items pulled from New York's garbage stream into our building and thus nicknamed The Scavenger; he always has a kind "have a great day have a great day" or a "how you doing how you doing" for me as I smile and stand to the side of the stairs listening to his endless greeting that I see as a ruse to prevent me from questioning the fact or otherwise admitting to myself that I never actually see him take any garbage *out*.

We are reminded of his presence whenever we find water dripping from our light fixture in the bathroom, which, thanks to our rather active imaginations, leads us to create frightening scenarios of the upstairs escapades taking place as well as filling our heads with visions of while-we-sleep flood, fire, and electrocution at the careless hand of our pack rat of a neighbor. Investigating the leak results in a confrontation between my roommate and The Scavenger, who invites her into his strange winding maze of an apartment, with accumulated detritus piled high to the ceiling and arranged to create little passageways lined with newspapers, magazines, and street garbage and leading to the bathroom—itself not so much an actual room in an apartment as an open chamber within an urban cave, a lesser cell within a human ant farm—where The Scavenger thinks the problem must be originating from. My roommate, worried about a clear escape route to the front door—or, for that matter, ever leaving The Scavenger's apartment alive again—is not only coping with the present and

obvious signs of The Scavenger's forgetfulness in terms
of turning off the bathroom taps, which is clearly causing our current internal rainshower activity, but also
with the evidence of Scavenger Man's lack of basic
hygiene, which flashes her back to a rather unfortunate experience months before I moved in when the
bathroom ceiling caved in on her in a *Carrie*-like shower
of excrement-soaked plaster.

The three of us find ourselves on a countdown to Des-
perate Living a few months later when the landlord
levies some shamefully ridiculous lease-renewal sum. I
halfheartedly entertain the idea of moving with one of
my roommates to an apartment over that French restaurant in the meatpacking district, visions of headless
cattle dangling from gambrel sticks and the stench of
gutters running with blood not exactly filling me with
Great Anticipation even though today it is quite the fashionable neighborhood. Meanwhile my French boyfriend
finally deserts his City of Light and arrives stateside
despite my non-penthouse budget that barely allows me
to sublet a dark apartment on Avenue A that leaves me
just as reluctant new-nabe-wise as the idea of my
vegetarian self living among the abattoirs of the West

Village. Alphabet City—Avenues A through D east of First Avenue—was for the longest time a decidedly off-limits zone, tucked as it is into the subwayless Lower East Side, where succeeding waves of immigrants had moved into a neighborhood hard-pressed to shake its history of anarchism, sweatshops, and unventilated tenement living spaces, with bathtubs in kitchens, bizarre apartment layouts, and other residential vagaries. This neighborhood of formerly cold-water flats, rechristened the East Village—in the same way that real estate brokers have given marketing facelifts to other formerly "unlivable" areas such as Hell's Kitchen–now–*Clinton*—has sprouted boutiques and fashionable eateries, out-of-place Gap stores and Starbucks coffee shops; but despite the closing of clubs and hangouts that don't jibe so well with the oddly new-and-improved residential neighborhood, and similar facade-deep attempts to change the nabe's image, the once-Loisaida nonetheless remains the Mediterranean Avenue of the New York real-estate Monopoly game.

The boyfriend meets the challenge of a new city and a new language, despite our barred-window one-bedroom apartment, junkies in the courtyard, gunshots at four in the morning, and assorted *final* final straws that include a friendly warning on the door from a neighbor asking us to "kindly disregard any strange noises" that might issue from her apartment since she will be bathtub birthing her baby any minute now; the visit from my friend Robyn that sees us unable to leave the building because the doorway is a yellow-tape roped-off murder scene complete with dead body and curious crowd; and the realization that the money we pass on to the junkie friend-of-a-friend we sublet from is not in point of fact ever received by the landlord, leading to a Sheriff of New York–delivered eviction notice, along with visions of a ten-gallon hat and chaps–wearing urban law enforcement official that I didn't even know *existed* padlocking and chaining our door in the days to come as I lie awake at night not especially eager to hear the imminent sounds of a different kind of special delivery issuing loudly from down the hall.

Moving

Horrorscope: A new branch of existentialism will come into being based on your life.

Through a combination of luck coupled with forlorn persistence we chance upon a first-floor one-bedroom apartment *avec* concrete backyard garden in Williamsburg, Brooklyn. The building itself is not so much brownstone as white clapboard, with the inside painted that uniquely hideous shade of 1970s-era burnt umber. Faced with the prospect of hiring a moving company I decide that it will most likely be cheaper for me to move us in my father's pickup truck, despite my rather not-impressive track record with driving vehicles belonging to my father, and ignoring the fact that if there is anything that terrorizes me more than being in a car accident, it is *almost* being in a car accident in my father's car and *living to tell him about it*, as revealed by my ability during my years of drivership to bring crippled cars of all descriptions hundreds of miles back home—

often at five miles per hour—through sheer willpower alone, rather than risk calling my father on the phone to tell him his car broke down at some outermost exit of the Parkway or Turnpike. Of course, when I make my thrifty move-it-myself decision I am unaware that a week later I will have chalked up hundreds of dollars in terms of expenses, counting gas, tolls, moving violations—one for going no more than two miles an hour through a red light north of Canal Street, more like a "barely moving" violation, and the other because my driver's license was packed away somewhere since I was, in fact, "moving"— and parking violations, witnessed by the half-peeled-off residuum of the fluorescent yellow THIS-CAR-PREVENTED-US-FROM-PROPERLY-CLEANING-THIS-STREET stickers representing thirty-five dollars each, that the street sweepers plastered over most of the pickup truck's windows, and that effectively block most of my view out of the truck while simultaneously sparing the officer-in-question the sight of me with my head on the steering wheel uncontrollably weeping over the incomprehensibly arduous task of trying to move basically from one side of the Williamsburg Bridge to the other.

Driving up the New Jersey Turnpike on what I

believe will be Moving *Day*, singular, I envision things
definitely on the upswing: we've found an apartment
that is on the up-and-up except for the illegal broker's fee
we pay to the friend of the landlord we deal with in
signing our lease; the boyfriend has managed to find
work with a tiny hair salon in Manhattan—the Brazilian
owner of which burns herbs Santeria-style in the bathroom and gives the boyfriend's starting-out English a
slight Portuguese inflection—and with a couple of trips
back and forth between Manhattan and Brooklyn we will
be home free. My attention is diverted, however, by a
mattress tied with what appears to be fishing line if not
sewing thread to the roof of the overpopulated car in
front of me, the faces inside pressed against glass. With
the mattress flapping rather disconcertingly up and
down with each bump of the car, I think to myself that I
wouldn't want to be behind that car when the mattress
flies up into the air and into traffic; the actual thought "I
wouldn't want to be behind that car when the mattress
flies up into the air and into traffic" forms in my head
just at the moment when the mattress flies up and falls
onto the Turnpike and under my father's pickup truck.

A reflex glance in the rearview mirror reveals

fortunately that no one is behind me as I slam on the brakes, as a hideous dragging noise audibly evidences that the mattress is now one with the truck and won't come unstuck as I pull over to the side along with the mattress's owner. A near-death-experience-derived calm overtakes me, and I stare straight ahead, not so much *at* the obscenely oversized car now parked in front of me but *through* it, as I attain some Zen-and-the-art-of-automobile-accident next level of consciousness.

To the sides of me I notice the driver of the car walking toward me, I notice the rubbernecking drivers on the Turnpike, I notice the other-car occupants seemingly perplexed by my resolute catatonia in the face of what happened. The driver approaches me and looks under the truck as I gaze calmly ahead, but instead of asking how I am, or otherwise inquiring into my well-being, all he manages to say is: "Damn! *It's ruined!*"

My demeanor must have changed at this point since he takes a step away from the truck—he chooses to step back into possible traffic rather than stand close to me—as my face now registers my anger not over almost getting killed in a car accident at the hand of the man standing next to me, but at *almost* getting *my father's pickup truck* in a car accident, while the damage-causing agent himself is more concerned with his almost-murder-weapon of a *mattress*. Without looking at him I put the car in reverse as calmly as I am able, and then floor the gas pedal, ripping the mattress to shreds and throwing up a cloud of stuffing and rent ticking, and I stick my head out of the window and yell: "No! *NOW* it's ruined!" as I drive away.

Brooklyn

Horrorscope: Everyone will come to claim their furniture that you found on the street.

Once we're in Brooklyn our connections to Manhattan include the L-stands-for-late subway train—the access to which one entire summer requires me to walk past construction workers eating lunch on Bedford Avenue who catcall "dolly!" (or, perhaps, "Dolly!") as I walk by, with one of them defending me for not looking "like a queer," which leads to a mixed feeling of relief and anger at the issues that such a statement brings up but which can't exactly be debated with putatively straight construction workers who, in any case, will think nothing of going home and watching football, or professional wrestling, or bodybuilding competitions, or war movies, or *Deliverance*, or a Henry Rollins concert, or any other half-naked sweaty male-on-male high-impact visual stimulation— and the Williamsburg Bridge, a not-confidence-building structure that seems at times to be held together by the silver paint splashed on it every year in a gratuitous attempt to make it appear physically capable of carrying four lanes of traffic, two subway tracks, and a pedestrian walkway. It is over this treacherous trail that I commute to work—via a bicycle that I buy at a police auction and that I imagine to be haunted by the messenger most likely run down while riding it, based on its beat-up condition. The trip is not eased by the huge sections of the walkway that are completely warped and uneven if not missing altogether; those cyclists in racing shorts and helmets tearing up the bridle path in Central Park on their thousand-dollar bikes and getting an adrenaline rush out of charging over molehill-sized mounds of wood chips at negligible speed have absolutely nothing at all on me, helmetless and maneuvering my way among the bridge's missing steel plates, looking down through the breaks in the walkway to the latticelike metal-grating road below, through which I can see straight down to the river flowing hundreds of feet underneath me, leaving me shaken up mentally as well as physically before my work day has even *begun*.

The initial incline from the Brooklyn side necessitates that I walk up to the midsection of the bridge when crossing, leaving me a bit winded when I haven't even started riding yet, and as I scan ahead to see who might be sharing the bridge with me I certainly never expect to see a metal door almost hidden in the riveted bridge structure open up, as it does during one indelible traversal-slash-action-adventure, as ten people file out from within the depths of the bridge's metal framework, popping up like living arcade-game opponents who at first glance I think might be repairmen, an impression contradicted by the fact that they are walking in zombielike slow motion, at which point I deduce that they are in fact drug addicts. I panic for an instant, since I am obviously outnumbered, but then relax when I realize that they are wasted on *smack* and not *crack*, since I can, if need be, outpace blissed-out heroin addicts; this leaves me perhaps for the first time in my life actually *relieved* to see a bunch of *junkies*.

Williamsburg is a nice enough neighborhood; my ride home takes me through the Hasidic, Hispanic, Italian, and Polish sections of town, or down by the as-yet-undeveloped waterfront that provides a spectacular view of Manhattan along with tugs and barges making their way down the East River. More intriguing landmarks include the near-empty light manufacturing and garment industry buildings, which still house a few determined floors full of whirring and shuttling machinery and are covered with signs in Spanish recruiting day laborers, and the factory by McCarren Park made out of corrugated tin whose logo portrays a rainbow going from yellow to orange, with workers bustling around outside in clean suits leaving yellow footprints wherever they go, and which, as far as I can tell from the yellow powder dusting the outside of the building where the roof meets the walls, produces the color yellow itself.

For the next two and a half years the boyfriend and I play "the nice boys next door" to our protective would-be aunts Grace and Rose—the Brooklyn equivalent of French *concierges*—who know everything about the comings and goings of the neighborhood and who inform me if someone has come by looking for me when I wasn't home, or if the monstrous ailanthus trees pushing through the cracks of the concrete basketball court that is our backyard need pruning, or if someone needs to tell my upstairs neighbor that her motorcycle has leaked motor oil on the sidewalk out front *yet again*, in a manner not-quite-meddling yet impossible to ignore.

They have an extraordinary repertoire of surveillance techniques—not to mention housedresses—and they listen attentively to my complaints about being the de facto super of the building, baby-sitting the oil furnace in the basement that has an annoying habit of temperamentally going out every other day; about the three apartments' worth of electricity that is hooked up to the one meter in the building, mine; and about the pool table that I now regret having helped the former upstairs tenants move in and that I swear will come crashing down on us as we sleep, as their three-o'clock-in-the-morning billiard tournaments are re-created real-time in my mind and my bloodshot wide-open eyes follow the paths of the clacking and rolling balls in the pitch dark.

Our one-stop-from-Manhattan neighborhood, formerly a world away, eventually starts to take on a decidedly hipster flair as East Village People migrate across the river in search of lofts and cheaper rents. The northside night-lit softball games of McCarren Park stand in ironic contrast to the southside art happenings and gallery openings where the newly arrived all-in-black crowds meld with the already-all-in-black Hasidim. Nonetheless we still miss Manhattan, which for being so close, might as well be hours away for the psychological barriers posed by the subway and the bridge—huge looming wonders of engineering originally devised to connect, but which, truth be told, end up separating quite definitively—and upon hearing of an apartment in a friend's building on the Upper West Side we decide to move out, pulling that keep-the-deposit-as-last-month's-rent maneuver that landlords love so much, and having learned our lesson actually call in a moving company to handle what we hope will be a quick getaway one Saturday morning without the landlord finding out. We underestimate Grace, of course, stealthily observing us from her second-story window.

"You moving?" she asks.

I shrug. "Yeah."

"Where to?" she wants to know.

"Back to Manhattan," I reply.

"To a nice neighborhood?" she asks, slightly defensive.

"We think so. . . . We'll miss this one, though," I add truthfully, but more for her benefit.

"Okay—I don't want to have to worry about you boys," she says resignedly.

I smile. We finish up packing and loading everything

into the truck, which goes on ahead as we head resolutely to the subway. We look up; Grace is still there. I
shrug and smile wanly. She gives us that one-handed-
shrug-with-eyes-closed-and-eyebrows-raised gesture. We
wave goodbye, and then feel vaguely sad as we walk
away. On the Manhattan side, the moving men shake us
down for a heftier tip, which I chalk up to landlord
karma.

The Building

For some reason the cinema portrays diary keeping as a sign of mental illness, like in the great documentary Crumb *where they are talking to R. Crumb's brother who shows the comix he used to draw and his notebooks that he used to graphomaniacally write and write in, his handwriting going from actual words written in tiny tiny cursive script to little scribblings that just look* like *writing; or in the movie* Seven, *when they enter the killer's dark and gloomy and badly lit apartment looking for clues and they find a room with bookshelves all over with Mead composition books filled with tiny tiny printing stacked everywhere, with long, slow pans around the murderer's room showcasing all of the bookshelves and notebooks all over the place obviously connecting a psychotic mind and writing things down, and all I can think as I'm watching the movie is: UM, THAT'S EXACTLY WHAT MY ROOM LOOKS LIKE!*

Our upper Upper West Side apartment comes thanks to our friend Robyn, who lives in the building and stakes out a newly available unit, conveniently ignoring the hospital bed still in the bedroom that belonged to the now-deceased former tenant and giving truth to the legend that the New York housing situation forces people to do things like read the obituary columns for real estate reasons. She herself now lives downtown, ironically enough, and I argue with her all the time that the rents Upper West Side–wise are exactly the same as the rents down her way (where we used to live years ago), but that in my new neighborhood views from restaurants don't include post-Tompkins-Square-Park-concert car overturnings, that apocalyptic postindustrial blight is not considered an interior design motif, that my garbage actually gets taken away *on a regular basis*, and perhaps most of all and mostly subconsciously, that I'd rather live uptown and seem *young*, than live downtown and seem *old*.

In contrast to the cramped quarters of apartments from our old neighborhood, we now have a long hallway that reminds me of my grandmother's apartment, where my father grew up and where we as kids were constantly yelled at for running up and down since it bothered the neighbors, which probably explains the stipulation in our new lease that the floors need to be carpeted. I bring along the Persian rug that was in my room at my parents' house and was actually broken in by trucks on the dusty streets of pre-post-Shah Abadan, Iran, where my father worked for a petroleum company before I was even born, and that I've taken with my father's blessings since he and my mother have already started packing and otherwise preretirement disencumbering themselves of their belongings. Every time I talk to my father on the phone he tells me about the books he's donating to the library or the papers he brings to the office to shred or my brother's comics that are still in his closet or my other brother's sofa that is still in the garage or my stuff that is also still in the garage, all of which needs to go before they sell the house. It always ends with us arguing about comparative quantities of accumulated stacks of stuff, parents' versus children's, and about who exactly he thinks we learned this Amassing Behavior from *in the first place*.

Only now everything they own has to go since they have their whole New Mexico–bound minimalist moving adventure mapped out, their allotment of kept objects not including the above-mentioned Persian rug that my father insists I take, or the china that my mother describes in historic detail while washing holiday dishes, offering me this or that piece despite my protests that I cannot think about the house we grew up in not being *ours*, much less deal with her giving away all of her generationally handed-down china *before they've even left*, or the actual worth-money objets d'art that my father funnels to Sotheby's for appraisal—like the statuette given to his father while working at the Plaza Hotel and now being auctioned off, the buyer-to-be in the dark concerning the fact that it used to be a doorstop in my grandmother's apartment; or the aborigine bark painting that was supposed to go to my brother who was born in Australia and that I am sure will result in my father's expatriation Down Under for crimes of absconding with indigenous artifacts. The whole situation is not unlike some warped archeological dig among the detritus of people who happen to *still be alive*, with the catch being that once we finally agree to take something—like the Persian rug, or the vinyl records my father has painstakingly catalogued—we then must deal with a stolen-from-my-grave guilt trip as if we have decamped with the family heirlooms, such as the Persian rug that my father is now convinced I took without asking, or the valuable albums that my father insists I'm *taking* from him like a riotous looter, despite my offer to actually *pay* for them, and which were, in fact, *pawned off on us in the first place.*

Like my grandmother's old apartment building, ours is a prewar structure—one that, in many ways, looks decidedly *après guerre* in terms of peeling paint and cracked plaster and the falling piece of ornamental stonework that almost did in a pedestrian, bringing about the removal of the entire decorative cornice of the building. Due most likely to the fact that we live outside the bounds of the local historic landmark district, the landlord is not required to precisely and historically-accurately rebuild the elaborate cornice, so he opts to have it unceremoniously jackhammered off instead, nearly causing my ceiling to cave in, and making me realize that certain stylistic architectural elements are nice to have—Bauhaus notwithstanding—since now the building looks like a pie with the fluted edge picked off. No one considered that removing tons of brick and mortar might cause the building to resettle, but of course it has, creating major fault lines in the walls and ceilings of every single apartment inside but especially those on the uppermost floor, like ours.

That same week we are notified that they are replacing the motor in the elevator, which is to be closed for two days—not a big deal unless you live on the seventh floor and have to walk your dog three times a day, which I do, and not a problem at all for people who prefer to get their exercise by doing a real-life StairMaster routine just to get home, which I definitely *do not*. After the motor is replaced I expect to sense a difference; I halfway anticipate the elevator will speed up or something, which it doesn't. But every so often I do perceive the mildest of tremors—the building vibrates for about ten seconds— and they definitely have the Dopplerish feel of a train going by, or of a mild earthquake. Not that I know from mild earthquakes, but I have a Special Phobia devoted to seismic events that I've never in my life even *experienced* that manifests itself when I go to visit friends in San Francisco and I envision earthquakes hitting just as my plane touches down, as if death by only *one* disaster isn't already more than enough; or when I walk downtown and I calculate the number of feet of shattered glass I'd be buried under based on the height of the buildings surrounding me; or when I try to determine, in some ridiculous mathematical branch of Cataclysmic Geometry of my own devising, how fast I would have to run under an overpass to escape being crushed under tons of highway concrete were an earthquake to hit as I start to walk under it; or when I stare fixedly and paralyzed with fear at the signs in the BART trains illustrating how to exit if you are in the Berkeley Hills when an earthquake hits, which is different from how you are supposed to exit if you are under the Bay when an earthquake hits, which is different from how you are supposed to exit if you are on an elevated track when an earthquake hits, as if I am supposed to be able to remember all of that once I'm post-Armageddon thrown into the debris-strewn darkness.

The quivering building unnerves, if only because there isn't too much rhyme or reason to the occurrences, so I quiz all of the neighbors, asking as composedly as I can whether they have noticed that the *entire building* trembles from time to time. One neighbor suggests that maybe they moved the subway over from Broadway to Amsterdam Avenue without telling anyone, while another thinks that the now cornice-less building is heaving a final sigh of despair before disintegrating into a pile of rubble with us on top. I, on the other hand, have rounded up my own suspects, such that whenever I feel the tremors begin I obsessively drop whatever I am doing and run out into the hall to see whether it is the elevator and its new motor, which it isn't, and then I run to the back of the apartment to look out the window to see whether it is the trucks on Amsterdam Avenue, which it isn't either. Days of anguish later, my friend Marjorie—to whom I complain about the vibrations fifty times a day— informs me that she has found the epicenter: it seems that the laundromat on the first floor has recently installed a shiny stainless steel space-shuttle-engine- driven spin-dry machine, which they bolted with little forethought to the foundation of the building. With all that the building has suffered, someone has unthinkingly attached the Kenmore equivalent of a four-point-five Richter-scale earthquake to its foundation, with the pleasure of knowing that for fifty cents and the luxury of spun-dry laundry, the infrastructure of an entire apartment building is literally being shaken *to its very core.*

Street Life

Once I was at Nadine's restaurant and there was a fund-raiser for Ann Richards of Texas politics fame. Her supporters were loudly carrying on and calling themselves "Texans in New York," as witnessed by these pins they were wearing, reflecting perhaps the one group of people whose collective sense of Self is not eclipsed by New York City's overwhelming Stadtgeist. At one point, one of the campaign workers stopped all conversation restaurantwide and said: "Excuse me, but Governor-to-be Richards is going to talk; would y'all mind being quiet for a few minutes?" There was a beautiful split-second only-in-New-York "fuck you" pregnant pause; then everyone went back to talking. Even louder than before.

Half of my time and energy as a New Yorker is given to keeping all aspects of the outside world *outside*, to such a degree that it might seem as if I were manning the walls of some medieval fortress, the only difference being that the Goths, and the Huns, and the other marauding hordes of centuries past had nothing on, say, those restaurant guys who shove menus under your door. I can honestly say that some of the more desperately ridiculous moments in my life have seen me yelling at the top of my lungs at some poor foot soldier in the army sent out by neighborhood restaurants who stuffs menus under everyone's door despite warnings, threats, and lawsuits; whose knowledge of the English language is often limited to the words he uses to gain access to the building— "UPS! Con Edison! Food delivery!"—and who, more often than not, just stares at me with bemused used-to-it-ness as I perform my unique brand of histrionic street theater. This would be quite absurd anywhere else but makes perfect sense in this city, itself invasive by nature, whose residents are extremely protective of personal space and are constantly made aware of their quality of life or lack thereof: if it's not the building shaking itself to pieces, then it's someone yelling up to "Delta" across the street to throw down the keys sixty times a day, or the merengue music that comes blaring out of car stereo systems that rival the power consumption of the cars themselves, or the pointlessly useless car alarms that go off whenever a demuffled motorcycle goes by. Day in and day out I personally would like to strangle the circuit-board jockey who soldered the first car alarm together with its to-distraction memorizable sequence of sleep-reducing squeals and honks; I pray for a branch of the police force devoted to apprehending woofer-powered automobiles; I wish that Delta would get a goddamned beeper already.

The other extreme of my guardian mode is much more sentinel-like. I spend entire days on the phone with my friend Judy downstairs, the two of us barely four vertical feet away from each other, complaining about the drug dealing and other goings-on in the street below during the '80s crack heyday; pathetically enough we fight over who gets to give the beleaguered Crack Hotline our over-rehearsed full head-to-toe description of the dealers brashly passing out crack below us, or we devise ways of getting rid of the crack addicts ourselves: water balloons from the roof is one idea, eggs another. Our respective partners disavow knowledge of us as we run down a list of the criminal activities witnessed that day, complete with nicknames for all of the now-familiar characters, embellishing the stories with each retelling as we cast ourselves as stars in a crime drama series of our own creation.

"Oh, listen to the crack birds!" I joke, attempting to shrug off the distinctive whistling the dealers use to call in their buyers. The endless whistling, along with the sweltering summer heat, eventually sends me over the edge, as I recall that a month earlier, when we were hanging a drug-prevention banner across our street warning buyers that this was a DRUG WATCH

NEIGHBORHOOD (more like a drug-obsessed pair on the two uppermost floors of the corner building), the crusty NYPD detective who came by to help recommended covertly the purchase of an air rifle in New Jersey, winking and whispering: "Sometimes you gotta fight fire with fire." That night, under cover of darkness, I take a pair of scissors and duct-tape them open with a block of moth-repellent cedar between the blades, and I take big rubber bands and a piece of an old Converse sneaker and attach them to the scissor handles, and I take rocks from the trays of one of my plants and I merrily open fire with my homemade slingshot on a cornerful of crack addicts, who scatter, not knowing what brand of plague-of-hail justice is pouring out on them from above. I run joyous and proud into the living room to show the boyfriend my accomplishment. He looks at me, looks at my weapon of crass construction, and yells: "What are you, *MacGyver*???"

His unsupportive attitude deters me not as I comb the parks while dog walking for perfect round rocks to stock my arsenal, and a perfect forked tree branch to make a perfect Dennis the Menace–style slingshot, with the ensuing adrenaline-pumping punishment that rains down from my apartment window keeping my lone corner of the world crack-free, until an errant shot explosively shatters the glass door across the street into a million tiny pieces and leaves me cowering on the floor of my bedroom with the lights out for the next few hours, awaiting the arrival of the investigating police who I know will eventually break down my apartment door. For days I avoid the elevator for fear of overhearing conversations about the horrible door-smashing incident, while upstairs in my room I shun my window knowing better than to Hitchcockily return to the scene of my crime. I actually get some work done for a change.

Later that week, eyes behavingly glued to my computer screen, I hear this loud booming noise like bombs falling, and despite my promise to myself and to the boyfriend that I will not waste my time getting upset at events happening outside my window and outside my control, the temptation proves too great and I pull back the curtain and notice that a resident in the halfway-house-slash-SRO across the street is lobbing things out of his window: bookshelves, a bike, cast-iron skillets; huge objects that I can't imagine fitting through his window *in the first place* are now tumbling down eleventh-plague-style onto the cars and stoop below. Unlike everyone who appears in those live-the-death television shows that appallingly re-create emergency experiences starring the selfsame people who already suffered through them once and who now relive for television the one time they called 911 in their lives, I somehow manage to call 911 at least once every other month; and also unlike those scary television shows featuring concerned caring heroic 911 telephone operators, I always manage to get New York 911 operators who could not possibly be more blasé, asking, "Where's the emergency?" as I give the coordinates of the crime scene, and then, "*What's* the emergency?" implying that it better be a good one.

"Yeah, there is this guy, like, throwing things out his window," I say, trying to portray the seriousness of what is going on with my voice but failing miserably. The operator pauses, and then replies as if disappointed, or rolling her eyes even, "*That's* the emergency?" as if I am wasting her time.

"No, like, really *big stuff* is coming out of his window! Chairs, and bikes, and *iron skillets*, and *bookcases* are *coming out of his window!*" I say, leaning on my window ledge and not getting a thing done as I proudly observe the closed-down street scene of my own creation for the next three hours.

Brunch

Topophobia: fear of particular locales.

—The Pill Book of Anxiety and Depression

Every Saturday morning for the past few years my friend Robyn has called me to ask about brunch; the fact of the matter is that we might as well just go to the exact same restaurant at the exact same time every Saturday, only that would be too simple. Every Saturday Robyn calls and says "what are you doing?" and I say "being woken up by a phone call" and she says "what are you doing today?" and I say "I don't know" and she says "you want to have brunch?" and I say "okay" and she says "where?" and I say "the exact same place we go every Saturday" and she says "what time?" and I say "the exact same time we have it every Saturday" and I don't think it is possible for two people in their midthirties to act more like ninety-year-old women whose only reason for living is to pester one another.

Our choice of restaurant is based on a process of elimination engendered by the exercise in apoplexy that is eating brunch on the Upper West Side, since the only thing my brain can focus on on Saturday morning is the provenance of my next cup of coffee, and I don't care how classy or trendy or swank the restaurant is as long as within two seconds of sitting down there is a waiter there asking me if I want a coffee—preferably with pot already in hand, if only to save precious moments of wasted uncaffeinated time. This was the modus operandi of all of those unglamorous diners with basic New York diner food on the menu that are now disappearing only to be replaced by the pretentious overpriced eating establishments that have cropped up of late, like that so-called café with its driving decorating paradigm of teddy bears and its hard inedible Yorkshire-pudding-looking so-called popovers and its new neighboring tchotchke shop and where lines of people wait outside to eat on the weekend; or that ersatz diner which takes the nostalgic *Happy Days* diner analogy and turns it on its Planet Hollywood head but which doesn't even stay open twenty-four hours and where lines of people wait outside to eat on the weekend; or that supposed pancake place whose one-item-menu dishes take inexplicable hours to prepare and where lines of people wait outside to eat on the weekend; or that barn-motif establishment with its dark tiny cramped can't-breath non-space with tables about one foot square and where lines of people wait outside for hours and hours in the freezing cold to eat on the weekend when right across the street is our process-of-elimination restaurant with its fish tank in the entrance where the food is okay and which has ample seating and no lines and where my biggest requirement of a brunch establishment is met week in and week out: normal coffee right away.

Usually brunch goes without a hitch: we arrive, we argue about sitting inside or out—I prefer the dark interior to the glass-covered exterior on the sidewalk where people walking by can stare in and watch me eat like some terrariumed zoo animal, or even worse, the tables set up outside where people walking by can not only stare and watch me eat, but could, if they so chose, lean in and *touch my food*—but sometimes it doesn't, in which case I wait restlessly for Robyn to arrive so we can promptly leave. These brunch-deserting hitches include parties of twenty waiting to be seated, or rambunctious sports fans at the bar providing color commentary heard restaurantwide, or crowds of shiny happy Upper West Side couples and their precocious children assembled en masse, who remind me of a television documentary on serial killers with the basic theory being that Children Are Evil until morals are instilled in them but some grow up and Stay Evil and commit mass murder, or assassinate people, and how the United States is the only country where assassinations are attempted not for political reasons, but because sick deranged minds want to get *Jodie Foster's attention*. My mood one crowded afternoon is further soured by my visit two days before to the periodontist to see about a pre-crown gum procedure involving grinding bone and cutting gum tissue; the disconcertingly overeager periodontist's following patient had canceled, leaving me to decide whether to have the procedure done right away. This seemingly simple request has unleashed a complex and multi-leveled decision-making process in my mind, due mostly to my habit of mapping medical procedures to those I've seen on television—not on *ER*, or *Chicago Hope*, or *St. Elsewhere*, but on the true-to-life *The Operation* on the Learning Channel, which I watch if only to get a glimpse of what might happen to me if I should need to go under the knife under similar circumstances, and which disappoints me immensely when they show inapplicable-for-me operations such as cesarean sections. Things are mildly complicated by my collection of medical reference texts, such as my *Stedman's Medical Dictionary* and my *Physician's Desk Reference* and my *Mosby's Medical, Nursing, and Allied Health Dictionary*, along with companion volumes given to me as presents by joking friends, such as *The Pill Book of Anxiety and Depression*, which leave me greatly not amused, mostly because I don't trust medical books that come out in miniature paperback editions weighing less than fifty pounds. The various doctors in my life do not at all appreciate my medical dabbling, due most probably to the exorbitant cost of acquiring an actual medical degree, as opposed to, say, the price of a couple of medical reference books, which lead me to provide final diagnoses instead of symptoms on the occasions when something goes wrong, with hours of pre-call research leading to preemptive statements, such as: "I think it's Bell's palsy," to the boyfriend's doctor, or "It's congestive heart failure complicated by pulmonary edema," to the dog's veterinarian.

Ninety-nine percent of such diagnoses are rejected in an objective prescreening process conducted on the phone with my mother, who deals with me in the same way she dealt with us kids when we tried to fake sick: she would demand evidence, preferably of a physical nature (due perhaps to her love of mystery and crime drama novels), staying one step ahead of our inventiveness like some sleuthing medical Miss Marple, foiling the majority of our attempts to stay home and watch cartoons all day. Currently she provides instant medical relief when I call home complaining of bad headaches and a stiff neck, for example, and saying, "Mom, I think I have spinal meningitis," and she matter-of-factly responds: "Dan, if you had spinal meningitis you would be in the hospital, most likely in a coma." Or, when I call her after a rigorous set of X rays at the dentist leaves me with a headache that won't go away, convincing me I have been radiographically overbombarded, and complain, "Ma, I had all these X rays done, and I think I have radiation poisoning," my mom's nonchalant desire for physical proof cures me instantaneously: "Well, Dan, *is your hair falling out?*"

Equally reassuring to me is *The Operation*: here is the

human body, here are the problems, here's how we fix them—unlike the more disturbing shows dealing with the enigma of the brain, like the PBS show about a woman's grand mal epilepsy and the quest to cut her brain to stop her seizures and the need to know what they would be cutting leading them to prod and poke with electrodes to see where her language center was, with the post-op recuperation tests consisting of the word "Jell-O," which she can write down, and the meaning of which she can describe like a contestant on *The $25,000 Pyramid*: "It's green, and clear, and shakes ...," but which she can't *say* in her strangely Ionesco-ish conversations with her doctor, as they both stare at her quivering translucent semantically nonexistent uneaten dessert. *The Operation* gives me a methodical banal backstage look at medicine, misrepresented by most of the emergency-room fare on television, but leaving me in my periodontist's chair imagining the show I saw where a girl gets her upper and lower jaws detached from her face to correct her overbite as they remove her upper wisdom teeth on a *whim* from the root end *up* as opposed to the teeth end *down*; but I agree to get it over with. Afterward I'm left with stitches; a huge flat piece of some Silly Putty–esque substance to protect the area (the dentist informs me this piece will fall off of its own accord—which has me worried I will choke on it in my sleep); a warning not to eat hot foods; and large amounts of Great Pain and waning patience as I wait for Robyn to show up.

The only place I'll agree to go, because I've never been there before, is another so-called café right down the block, which is aiming for that street-level Euro-café feel with its huge wood-framed windows even though it's up one flight of stairs, and in true Euro-style no one meets us inside asking how many we are, and when we finally sit down no one is giving us silverware, and no one is giving us water, and no one is waiting on us or otherwise giving us coffee, making my already-bad mood even worse. The woman next to us is discussing how her vet just scraped out the inside of her dog's ears, which is revolting to begin with, as I realize that the menu, broken down into stereotypical ethnic breakfasts (Viennese, Dutch, Greek, English), coupled with my soft-food dietary requirement, leaves me an Irish breakfast of oatmeal, only after listening to the dog-ear-scraping story oatmeal is right off. Instead I decide on the "Belgian" waffles, not really ever having gotten the whole "Belgian" part of that particular waffle equation, it always seeming to be one of those country names that get attached to the name of a food without any relevance to the actual originating country, like French vanilla, or French toast, or French fries, making the by-country breakdown of the café's menu all the more ridiculous; but even worse, the thought of Belgian waffles produces scary visions of Karen Finley, the once–performance artist now found more often in the laid-back lifestyle sections of *The New York Times*, best known formerly for smearing her body in chocolate and introducing food-stuffs into her various orifices, which she then sings about in songs with lyrics such as "I've got Belgian waffles in my twat"; and I think it would be fair to say she has single-handedly done more to stem the consumption of chocolate sauce, and yams, and Belgian waffles than anyone else in the entire world. We order our food and wait for our this-better-be-damned-good $1.75 cups of "regular coffee."

"Coffee" falls into that retrofitted word category of things that used to be described by one word but now have to be called "regular" because someone made them trendy, with "regular coffee" now used to describe just plain coffee as differentiated from all of the new categories of coffee that exist. This fact was brought home to me most vividly during a trip to San Francisco where my New Jersey/New York mentality has me searching the greater part of the day for a simple diner-like establishment with a counter where I can order a fifty-cent coffee, and finally settling on a café, since I am at the end of my ability to walk anymore, San Francisco maps neglecting to show critical details such as elevation, for example, and I am not helped by this café, which doesn't seem to have chairs, or stools, or anything to sit on as I ask: "Can I just get a regular coffee please?" I am perplexed by the café-girl's response of: "We don't serve *coffee*"—which, I hasten to remind her, is all that is listed on the huge menu on the wall behind her, bringing on the why-do-I-bother response of: "That's not *coffee*, those are *caffeinated beverages!*" Even worse, "regular coffee" already existed as a term, at least in New York, with its new meaning, "coffee that is not espresso-based," clashing with the old meaning, which now requires the not-at-all-succinct "regular coffee with milk," with my only recourse being to curse Seattle and the entire West Coast coffee culture for this mind-numbing state of affairs every time ordering coffee ends up taking huge chunks out of my day and I end up with a wrong coffee order *anyway*.

I get a look from the scraped-ear-dog lady next to me as I cool down my coffee with ice cubes, not wanting to inadvertently melt my Silly Putty, while menacing our other flank is a woman and her precocious girl-child. I should probably clarify that I love children, I love my role as Doting Uncle, and am not at all embarrassed shopping with the boyfriend for all manner of rather impractical miniature clothing ensembles—not to mention toys and books that I'd just as likely buy for myself—all the while loudly squealing delight over the unbearable cuteness of *kinderstuff*. But there is something upsetting about a certain generation's generally lackadaisical and psychobabbly way of bringing up its children, exemplified by a woman I saw with her child on a train coming into the city modeling-agency bound and incessantly brushing her boy's hair, with every request to "sit down" or "quiet down" bringing on her son's grabbing-the-reins-of-failed-reverse-psychology berating retort of: "You're yelling at me, *you're yelling at me!*" Or the mother I often run into at the day care center when I pick up my friend's son who, after a long hard day's work, hangs out for close to an hour asking her daughter, "Okay, do you want to go home yet?" All of this is in stark contrast to what I remember as a rather disciplined upbringing with precociousness not at all considered cute, but rather with emphasis on the fact that contrary to your selfish childish belief there were actually other children and other people besides you and you needed to share and you needed to not scream and you needed to not punch that other kid in the sandbox and you needed to understand that disobeying your parents brought *sure and swift punishment* of one kind or another, with this generation of parents perhaps reacting out of fear that children who are not spoiled, and not indulged, and who are not pampered nonstop will come down with some sort of kiddy psychosis, to then grow up and invent refund memories, recalling twisted of-Satanic-origin sexual misconduct on some psychotherapist's couch.

The woman sits down with her daughter, who is

whining about wanting her jacket on, and then wanting her jacket off, and then wanting it on and then wanting it off but it can't be on the chair, but she wants her Winnie-the-Pooh stuffed bear, as Robyn and I both channel our respective parents' decisive end-of-discussion statements via ESP in the hopes that the child might pick up our silent screams of: "Turn around and sit down right this instant!" The girl decides: "I want a coffee I want a coffee!" and the mother is not saying no, and when the waitress arrives, the mother orders a *coffee for the little girl*; before we can comment our food arrives with my Belgian waffles piled high with whipped cream in what is the most obscene breakfast dish in the whole Wide World of Breakfast Dishes served at this so-called café and which I have to squish around my mouth with my tongue since I can't chew, leaving everything tasting vaguely of Plasticine. Soon the food at the next table arrives, with the waitress saying, "I'll be right back with her coffee." The mother finally realizes that everyone within earshot is staring at her, and perhaps sensing that it is not beyond us collectively to call the child welfare authorities if need be—as I kick Robyn in the leg to prevent her from doing just that—the mother states loudly as the waitress returns: "What are you doing? Are you crazy? You can't give a child coffee!" which, as ridiculous a turnaround as it is, is much appreciated, since, as little in the mood as we are to put up with her child, we are even less in a mood to put up with her child *stoked on caffeine*.

Rodentia

The squirrel has become the daytime equivalent of the rat. For whatever reason, people feed squirrels, coax squirrels to approach them, and generally treat them with the exact opposite of the hate bestowed upon the rat. They are like those rotten little kids who, since they are so cute, can get away with anything. The squirrel is a cute rat, without the reputation.

When talking about survivors, adapters, and hangers-on, one is usually making reference to the more human inhabitants of this city, instead of the lower-on-the-genetic-totem-pole denizens sharing every square inch of the city with us: the stinking trees of heaven sprouting out of every atom of available soil; the filthy pigeons that people feel sorry for and feed in the winter—while paying no nevermind to the freezing-cold homeless people likewise scrounging for food and shelter on the streets—which then fly up and make disgusting pigeon-sex noises outside our windows, or roost on our windowsills, or ignobly expire on my friend Marjorie's bathroom window ledge leaving thousands of fly larvae crawling around her bathroom as calling cards when spring finally rolls around; or the huge waterbugs that come up through the shower drain and leave such an indelible impression that the boyfriend suffers a paranoid fit in imagining the keys in his pocket to be some huge insect crawling up his leg that causes him to strip off his shorts in the middle of the street—with my immediate concern not so much the possibility of bloodsucking hitching-a-ride vermin but the likely criminal charge of indecent exposure as reported by the people across the street currently watching his French Striptease; or the various subspecies of *Rodentia*, which as far as I'm concerned includes squirrels, along with the huge rats seen in the subway and the peripheral-vision-spied field mice that inhabit my building to such an extent that I wonder who is trespassing on whose turf sometimes, despite the fact that the nearest field is fifty-odd miles away.

Our running battle with mice has gone on for years—one particularly bad infestation made us consider simply replacing our plaster wall with a big piece of glass to at least be able to enjoy the Habitrail that is the wall separating us from the apartment next door. Their return is always heralded by the dog, who sniffs along the baseboard and the closet door or who all of a sudden tears into the kitchen on the scent of some tiny mouse prey; since the mice are in the walls and not yet in the apartment proper, I double-check our first line of defense, which is the steel wool filling every hole in every closet and the space around every pipe in the apartment, with the dog patrolling the baseboards like some moated crocodile searching for castle gate crashers.

Our defense system holds up pretty well, although the encroached fortress wall is revealed by the dog's barking, which is more than his usual heard-a-dog-barking-outside growling, and different from his saw-a-pigeon yapping; I go into the kitchen and turn on the light and behind the dog's food dish is a mouse, a brazen creature not scurrying away but just sitting there facing the food dish; I stand there a full few minutes and the dog stands there and the mouse stands there as well, and I try to think like a little mouse, which, like the creatures of that book *Flatland*, can't likely imagine something six feet tall staring down at it from above—which accounts for why the mouse facing the blue plastic of the dog's bowl probably considers itself well hidden. The mouse makes a break for it, narrowly escapes the dog now hysterically in Hunting Mode, and runs under the dishwasher, as the dog vigilantly paws the floor in front of the dishwasher until the mouse, a few minutes later, emerges, on its side, legs running in the air, bleeding a red streak across the linoleum, giving itself up before dying at the feet of my crazed dog, who I can only imagine now considers himself a Great Hunter.

Months go by, and we figure that our dog has done a good job of ridding us of this one mouse scout leaving the other mice in retreat, until the super puts a sign in the elevator announcing the exterminator's imminent visit to "deal with" the mouse problem; meanwhile the dog, sensing conflict perhaps, is again on the prowl, barking at the stove, and then at the refrigerator, and crying, and generally driving me crazy with his barking-at-major-appliance behavior, which turns out to be dead-on when I hear scratching coming from within the stove and I lift up the top and another mouse runs down into the oven as brilliant me turns on the gas but then, thinking of that book *Maus*, shuts it off, not because I was about to pull a Sylvia Plath due to vermin in the stove, but, more distressing to me, due to a comic-book interpretation of the Holocaust.

That night the dog decides to bark at the living room furniture instead of the kitchen appliances. Since I now trust his instincts, I gingerly move a cushion only to see a brief flash of mouse fur scurry inside the couch. Now, I'm pissed. After ten years of living with an in-no-way-comfortable futon the boyfriend and I finally invested in a nice couch; for ten years we argued about style, and fabric, and workmanship, and price every time we would actually make a point of going couch shopping, and since we managed to agree on this one style-, fabric-, work-manship-, and price-wise, I was not about to allow some Family Von Mouse to live inside as if it were some plush overstuffed rodent condominium. I break out the chemi-cal weaponry: mouse poison.

The next morning I wake up and stumble into the kitchen to make coffee with the dog at my heels to check the appliances, and then into the living room to check the furniture, and then into the bathroom where he almost does a cartoonlike somersault in that way dogs have of stopping their front legs while their back legs keep going, since there, on the floor, is the mouse from the previous day. I chase the dog away and throw the mouse down the garbage chute re-re-disposing of the monster; but later at brunch with Robyn when I relate the story to her she keeps correcting me: every time I say "mouse" she says "mice" and I say "mouse" and she says "mice" and finally she says: "What makes you think there is only one? Like, maybe it was an orphan or something?"

Another day goes by, and a weird smell pervades the kitchen which I figure is the not-taken-out garbage, or the not-taken-out recycling, and I throw everything away and I throw open the windows only to find the dog once again barking his fool head off; this time, however, a fly has managed to invade our air space; the dog is unable to get much traction on the wood floors, and does a pretty good Wile E. Coyote imitation of running in place as I hunt down the fly, just to get some peace and quiet. The boyfriend arrives home just then and joins the hunting expedition, which moves into the kitchen where we both stop, because like an *Amityville Horror* warning-to-leave, huge, bloated, repulsive flies have collected on the kitchen window screen. The boyfriend exclaims: "What is that smell! It's disgusting!" This bothers me, since it recalls for me the time we had a big fight and he brought home a bouquet of lilies that I later learned were a gift he'd received at work, and every night he would come home and loudly proclaim how nice his pawned-off-on-me guilt-gift of lilies smelled; since I could not detect any lily scent at all this prompted an entire new argument about whether the argument-appeasing-gift of lilies smelled or not, until to prove my point I stuck my nose point-blank in the bouquet and realized that, yes, indeed, lilies do smell; they stink in fact, of rotten cloves, or some other decomposing vegetation, making the secondhand present of lilies all the more *loathsome*.

Once again, the boyfriend smells something that I do not. I no longer have the excuse of the garbage, or the recycling; I start disassembling the dishwasher into the middle of the floor, a cue for the dog to attack from behind before I have a chance to see what is there; meanwhile the boyfriend, cigarette in hand, is quite blasé-ly calling his mother in France, watching me as I systematically dismantle the entire kitchen, using an actual unwieldy lamp from the living room to see since we don't have a flashlight to shine into the darkness behind the dishwasher, where the smell is appreciably worse, and where I can see the black bloated body of a dead mouse. I'm about to vomit. The boyfriend is not only not helping keep the dog at bay, he is giving a play-by-play commentary to his mother in French, including a description of the dog's desperately inane attempt to tunnel underneath the dishwasher, and then distracting me with his mother's questions concerning the state of the mouse—translated literally from the French as "What face does the mouse have?"—which makes me scrunch up my face and roll up my eyes in a feeble attempt at impersonating a dead rodent.

It is with all the will I can muster with a plastic trash bag turned inside out on my arm and with a wad of paper towels in my hand that I reach in, grab the mouse, and throw it down the trash chute in the hallway. I come back and look on the other side of the dishwasher and there's another dead mouse, so I go through my little trash bag pomp-less mouse-funeral ritual not just once but twice more, with the last mouse being a mummified forebear from years before, as if the dishwasher were a huge pyramid-esque burial ground. I throw out all of the poison behind the refrigerator, vowing to use regular mousetraps for any subsequent Mice Invaders, since the mice, in a final act of revenge, seem to pick the most inaccessible areas of the apartment to die in like wounded soldiers pulling themselves off of the battle-field, urging their compatriots on, in some strange War of Mousean Independence.

Dog People

New York City for a while had its own chocolate bar—called appropriately enough Nutty New Yorker—which wasn't too bad, although buying one was a bit disconcerting, like admitting you were in therapy or something.

Owning a dog in New York City reveals a strange other world of daily meetings with strangers and pedigree-based social orders, which humankind instigated bloody revolutions to be rid of but which live on in a certain kind of canine class distinction that comes in many forms. On the Lower East Side, in a neighborhood of menacing pit bulls with spiked choke collars held in check by stoopfuls of homeboys watching me make my way down the broken-glass-strewn streets with my Tasmanian-devil-looking tiny dog, I am hard-pressed to give off an air of toughness and coolness, even though there are people in the world who are in fact afraid of my dog, like a plumber who comes by because a leak in our bathroom brought the ceiling down downstairs and who puts a hole in the wall big enough for the dog to get through to the neighbors' apartment and who, spying my dog, asks me, "Can you hold your dog please?" even though I reassure him that "He won't bite," to which he nastily replies: "Listen, I got fourteen stitches from a dog once, and I don't care if it's a Chihuahua, I'm scared of dogs!"—with the Chihuahua remark irritating me above all else since while walking the dog one day past the above-mentioned stoop of homeboys my prayers not to be on the receiving end of any undue notice or biting nonaccolades that the dog thankfully doesn't understand are ignored as one of them yells: "YO! Check out the CHIHUAHUA with a *FRO!*" The Upper West Side, on the other hand, reveals a hierarchy not based on dog *machismo*, but rather on complicated Relative Breed Analysis formulas and Return on Canine Investment ratios, with parental-type conversations of day care, and doctor's bills, and childhood health problems, and school being replaced with their canine equivalents of kennels, and veterinary bills, and doggy health problems, and obedience training, the only difference being that a child eventually manages to grow up, leave the house, and *earn her keep.*

Riverside Park is overrun with dogs off the leash since for some twisted reason Dog People feel that canine rights supersede human rights, to the point that I don't understand why the non–dog owners have not risen up and banned dogs from that park once and for all. Every once in a while I see some new dog owner trying to join the Dog Elite alone in the middle of the park with his purebred-of-the-month puppy, waiting for people to come up and inquire about his Golden Retriever, or his Chow, or his Pug, or his Disney-derived Dalmation. One of the sadder trends in dog ownership concerns the broken-down greyhound adopted post-career, a skittish bag-of-bones paraded around as a sad testament to the altruistic nature of the owner who has "saved" the greyhound from being put down, such ownership garnering extra bonus points in the sympathy department, with a hidden bonus for the owner since the investment years-wise for a busted-up old greyhound that looks like it's going to kick the bucket *any second* is much less than for a regular dog obtained as a puppy.

I have not one smidgen of patience for people who ask about my dog, mainly because he is not a breed of any kind; in fact he looks more extraterrestrial than dog-related. My particular Toto-esque mass of wiry black fur was found on the streets of Paris, where he was left outside to perish, and then rescued by some students at the

American College who proceeded to name him "Chee-bai," which they informed everyone was Chinese for "vagina"; however, the novelty of a puppy soon wore off and I lobbied some mutual friends to talk them into giving him to me, partly because they were going to be returning to the States soon and obviously were only half-interested in raising him, but mostly due to my abject mortification at the thought of them screaming "Vagina!" in Chinese at the dog all day long. I renamed him Czaro since it was really difficult for French people to pronounce, such that half the people who knew him thought his name was *Zorro*, and also because I thought that "Czara" would make a nice dog's name, with "Czaro" being the unfortunate masculine equivalent. Czaro was my constant companion in Paris, where I could bring him with me on the subway, or to restaurants, or to work, as opposed to New York, where Czaro unfortunately spent most of his time inside, but at least forced me out of the apartment three times a day.

"What kind of dog is that?" is the question I most often get from people who either want to show how much they know about dog breeds by guessing at Czaro's lineage, or they want to talk about their own pedigree dog;

in either case they are quite disappointed when I answer, "Just a mutt," effectively stifling any continued conversation on the topic. The question I get next most often is more pointed: "Is that an Affenpinscher? Brussels Griffon? Cairn Terrier?" People asking this question get a kick out of watching the Westminster Kennel Club Dog Show, perhaps the worst display of human beings degrading themselves along with another species in its entirety. The first time I am so specifically asked Czaro's breed I am clueless as to what an Affenpinscher even is until later research reveals something closely resembling Czaro—or at least a clipped, groomed, bathed, less-demonic-looking version—at which point I conclude that Czaro, for all intents and purposes, will from now on *be* a purebred if people so want him to be. Friends scoff at the idea, and refuse to believe that anyone asks me that question or that anyone would believe my answer to be true in any case, but one by one they are disproved like my friend Robyn, who accompanies me to Riverside Park during one of New York's so-called Ten Best Weather Days, when the tide going out in the Hudson reveals that the ersatz marina boat basin at 72nd Street is actually a huge piece of concrete jutting out into the river and that its year-round residents, who have great pretensions of some seafaring lifestyle, are actually living on the equivalent of a parking lot where the sewers overflow. Robyn is halfway asleep on the blanket when I notice a woman making a beeline for us. I describe her movement under my breath like a spy discussing the advances of approaching troops: "Here she comes Robyn, she's still coming, she's almost here . . ." and the woman arrives at our blanket, looks knowingly at Czaro, and says: "Excuse me, but is that an Affenpinscher?" as Robyn's eyes shoot wide open and I reply, chest filled with avenged pride, "Why yes! Yes it *is* an Affenpinscher!"; or my friend Barbara, who goes with the boyfriend to walk Czaro in Riverside Park and one after another people ask her if Czaro isn't an Affenpinscher, or if Czaro isn't Molly, an *actual* Affenpinscher who lives in the neighborhood, or otherwise comment on how Czaro is *cute*. Barbara denies that he is an Affenpinscher, and denies that he is Molly, and denies that he is cute, and finally tells one woman: "He's a mutt dog from another planet!" at which point the woman leans in, almost afraid to be overheard, and confides: "Yes, but Molly's *weirder-looking*."

Every day is thus spent defending my dog's non-

purebred existence instead of simply walking quietly
in the park unhounded by off-leash dogs of very particular lineage who chase after poor tethered Czaro as
their owners' kids run after me yelling, "Hey stop so I
hey my dog I gotta get my dog hey stop so I can get my
dog"; or responding to questions such as from the woman
who owns a Brussels Griffon who makes a point of
inviting Czaro to her dog's birthday party but never says
whether I *myself* am invited as well, although I don't
dare ask since the image of party-hatted tiny dogs running around this woman's apartment is more than I can
handle; or averting undue attention from people like the
postal clerk who knows Czaro since I bring him with me
to the post office all the time and who opens up a line for
express/priority mail outside of the call-number system
as I am waiting patiently for it to arrive at my number,
only the postal clerk recognizes me and asks me to tell
people the line is closed after me, but my worry of people
going postal prevents me from informing any of the three
people now behind me in line that it is closed, since the
longer I wait the more outnumbered I am. I pray that my
number gets called at another window and I stare at the
number changer on the wall, which finally ticks over; I

leave the line and go wait on the other side of the post office as I hear this postal clerk, now realizing that I didn't in fact do my duty to tell anyone not to get in line, filling the post office with his cries of: "Father of Czaro! Father of Czaro! Come to window two! *Father of Czaro!*" I am so petrified that someone might think I answer to the name of "father of Czaro"—not to mention my fear at being chastised by a postal clerk—that I hide behind a stamp machine for a full ten minutes.

Pet Neurosis

Missing Bird: Reward

- *White with touches of coral and yellow*
- *Large bald patch on chest*
- *Smaller than a pigeon*
- *Scrawny*
- *NEEDS MEDICATION*

—Missing-pet sign found in Riverside Park

I'm not at all convinced that the city is a good place to raise animals, partly because of the physical constraints of tiny apartments and leashes in parks, but mostly because of the psychological trauma of an unnatural urban environment that drives zooed polar bears to sink into depression, cats to jump from apartment ledges, and pet owners to actually shell out money for pet psychotherapy. I had gone the extra mile when bringing Czaro home to find an airline that would allow me to bring him on board with me due to horror stories of dogs going crazy in the holds of planes during long flights and never seeming the same again, and knowing that Czaro probably didn't have too far to go I wanted to avoid any and all risk; on the day of the flight home I gave him his tiny tranquilizer that I didn't think was working until he cartoonlike suddenly keeled over, and then remained knocked out for the rest of the flight. As we were arriving in New York the mother of a crying child pointed to Czaro, now a stellar example of proper plane behavior, but she was not even slightly amused when I recommended the doggy-downer tranquilizers.

Having survived all of that, I find it extremely upsetting while pursuing my master's degree to discover that Czaro is suddenly acting strange, standing with his back arched and his front paws extended and not eating for days at a time. I take him to the vet, who does X rays and blood tests and other tests and says that he doesn't know what the problem is. I thank him and leave, since I can't really afford to pay so much to hear that he doesn't know what is wrong, but most importantly, because the man's clogs do not exactly inspire confidence.

I take Czaro to another clinic in the neighborhood since, as finals approach, his symptoms now include vomiting up blood. I go through the whole symptom list again, the vet thoroughly ignoring me as she lifts up Czaro's tail and declares, "Ah, Czaro still has his testicles!" and lifts up his lip and says, "Ah, Czaro is about due for a teeth cleaning!" in that childlike way of talking to pet owners that is patronizing yet understandable in light of how the average pet owner reverts to infantile goo-goo behavior once inside the walls of a veterinary clinic, with the irony of New York pet owners being rude and pushy to other *people* while they wait for the daily tubal feeding of their precious cockatoo totally lost on me in purely humanistic terms. I want to remind her that we are not here about his *teeth* and that there is no danger of Czaro *procreating* anytime soon and can we please just get on with the diagnosis part of the examination, which starts out wholly in left field with the question she then asks: "Are you under a lot of stress?"

"Um, do I live in New York City?" I reply, not exactly sure where she is going with this, to which she responds, "No, I mean *additional* stress."

I stop and think for a minute, never having before contemplated the concept of *additional* stress since I have never in fact divided my stress into hierarchies or categories or partitions of *main* stress versus *additional* stress, like a reserve gas tank full of stress that kicks in when the main tank of stress is *used up*. I offer the fact that I am in graduate school as one of the huge list of things that might be considered "additional," hoping she will accept that since anything else is going to get kind of personal.

"Well, I think Czaro is picking up on your stress and is manifesting it in a preulcerous condition."

I am so taken aback that I stare at her blankly for about two minutes. Meanwhile on the wall behind her are pictures of happy dog owners with their happy dogs, and thank-you notes from thankful pet owners to my vet for having saved Muffy and Binky and Sasha; and one of the pictures is from a smiling Sally Jessy Raphael with her dog, both looking down at me happy as can be, and I don't consider it very fair that my dog should have mental problems if Sally Jessy Raphael's dog doesn't. Finally I manage to say, "So basically you're telling me that my dog needs to take pills to treat *my* stress," as I logically conclude to myself: Why don't we just give the pills directly to *me*?

Per veterinary orders I switch barely-nine-pounds-anyway Czaro to a low-fat diet of specialty-brand dog food costing two dollars a can, which earns me strange looks from the pet store people when I show up with this scrawny dog and ask for the dietary dog food; their questioning looks are only surpassed by those of my pharmacist, who quizzes me concerning the quarter-tablet-twice-a-day seventy-dollars-a-bottle prescription of Tagamet that I hand him: "Is this prescription for you?"—to which I reply that no, it's for my dog, not wanting to let on that it is *my fault* that my dog has to take an expensive no-generic-equivalent ulcer-negating acid inhibitor, not to mention that I've spent more on my dog's health care than on my own. For weeks after, when people ask me how I am doing I testily reply: "I don't know, ask my dog!" Much later, whenever he starts showing symptoms again, I am forced to stop and take stock of my life, wondering what is wrong that I'm not aware of and pretending to be happy for the dog's sake since I really need Czaro to get better not only because it is sad to see him sick, which it is, but more than anything else because he is basically my *mental health barometer*.

Infrastructure

Only technology evolves.

—Graffito found on Irvington Street

New York City has always represented to me the true *Bladerunner*-esque future of cyberpunk prognostication. Unlike the hippies-turned-neo-cons of Cali-based *Wired* and other nouveau-technocratist rags with their big smiley-faced Gingrich-esque vision of a sparkling clean urban techno-utopia, I much prefer to look at the imposition of technology upon a constantly crumbling infrastructure such as New York's—with its venting steam pipes, exploding water mains, and rather rundown subway system—as representing the true future of what is now considered slick and shiny and problemless technological innovation. Given enough time, the constantly and irreversibly encroaching technology in our lives—the not-asked-for money-chip that is on my new ATM card, or the new camera in the lobby pointed at the front door that is hooked up to a channel on my cable service, or the

security surveillance installed in Washington Square—
will one day explode in our faces, the modern-age
equivalent of the asbestos geyser. The purveyors of new
technological innovation paint people like me as Lud-
dites and technophobes—like the so-called customer service lady at Time Warner Cable who spends ten minutes
telling me how *wrong* I am to want to downgrade my
cable service—despite our years devoted to school and
staying ahead of the much-heralded Information Age
that supposedly is just around the corner and that, years
and years later, I'm still waiting for while paying back
my overwhelming mountain of student loans. As far as
I'm concerned, anyone who entrusts the organization of
their lives to battery-powered gadgets and the entirety
of their personal communication to electronic devices is
quite deserving of those oddly exalted figureheads of the
New World Order whom I think of every day as I curse
every dehumanizing technical intrusion in my life, and
who don't mention to anyone that they, in fact, hire *other
people* to deal with their e-mail, and personal communications, and every other doubles-the-work aspect of their
wondrous future of Jetsonian metal and plastic.

I often stop to consider how much of my life is dedicated to not so much *using* technology as *dealing* with it: not *using* a VCR, but trying to get it to work with the various and sundry cables emanating from a separately programmed Time Warner Cable—required cable box and a stereo and an old 8-bit Nintendo game that a masters degree in interactive telecommunications doesn't at all help me to figure out; not *using* my ten-year-old Mac for any productive reason but calculating the vacation time that Apple Computer owes me for all of the accumulated hours I've stared at that little wristwatch icon telling me to *wait*; not *using* beepers or cellular phones but being forced to listen to other people's beepers going off and other people's cellular phone calls, knowing that while *live trees* are being cut down in virgin forests around the world, *fake trees* are being constructed to act as bases for cellular phone transmitters. I can't for the life of me fathom this desire to be more reachable, more attainable, more *in-touchable*, as halves of phone conversations fill my head at all times during the day even in places that should be off limits if only in terms of good taste and etiquette, like crowded restaurants, or trains, or movie theaters, or pretty much *anywhere* for that matter, but perhaps most especially the bathrooms down the hall from Cellular One in Rockefeller Center, where I was freelancing on the same floor and whose workers are not detached for one second from their cellular phones— including, to my great disgust, while *on the toilet*.

New Yorkers end up dealing with the wild side of their urban jungle whether they want to or not: streets ripped open to reveal the twisted innards barely contained below their feet, huge hidden electric transformers that make their humming presence known in the Walkmans worn to drown out audible-range street noise. The tech bites back in big ways sometimes, like the skyline-dimming blackout decades ago that left my father stranded at Penn Station, or in small ways, like on the first day in our new Upper West Side apartment that finds me plugging in our cordless phone and having it ring immediately regardless of the fact that we'd only actually been residents of our new apartment a scant few hours, a phenomenon made stranger by the simple fact that it is somebody else's phone conversation on the line, which makes me hang up; and this continues all afternoon as I go to make a call only to find there is someone on the line already, or I pick up the ringing phone and there is already someone on the line, and I decide to switch the channel that our phone is set to while listening to a phone conversation already in progress:

"So, what's that noise in the background?"

"I don't know; all I know is some cocksuckers moved into the building, and they *fucked up my phone!*"

I slam the receiver down, change the channel, and listen again, hoping beyond hope for a dial tone.

"Listen, missy, I didn't pay a hundred-fifty dollars for you to fuck up my phone!"

The boyfriend comes home later to find me blanched and shaking and putting in the old corded phone, which I use to this day, since in this crowded city crossed communications can be heard not only on cordless phones but on intercom devices like those cute multicolored baby-listening intercom gizmos and TVs that still have the old set of UHF channels on a separate dial and from which issue ghostly one-sided conversations. It's not even like my corded plug-in-the-wall phone is immune: the no-end-of-trouble phone line that had to be routed up from the basement outside the building over the roof and into my window since they removed the dumbwaiter-slash-phone-line-conduit during renovation also manages to transmit various voice communications other than the ones I listen to, like the radio chatter and Spanish car service radio banter piped to my ear by the de facto radio antenna that is a five-hundred-foot phone line; or the Spanish crosstalk on my line that has me listening to the dismembered voices of a numbers racket; or even WABC talk radio that means any given phone conversation finds me getting progressively angrier at the bone-headisms coming out of Rush Limbaugh's mouth and with the person I'm talking to completely oblivious to the one-sided radio broadcast that I'm privy to perplexed when our conversation U-turns into a political discussion or when I suddenly scream out: *"Did you hear what Rush Limbaugh just said?!"*

The notion of miscommunication reaches new heights with the answering machine, on which people who've dialed wrong numbers leave messages and have no idea that their pleas and questions and requests go unheard by the intended party who happens not to be us, leaving me anxious as to the outcome of their situations in a *Rear Window* soap opera-esque way, especially when they concern canceled plans or relationship-related back-and-forth, or are relayed in the cracking voice of a worried mother wondering why her child doesn't pick up, which leaves me completely crestfallen; not to mention those hang-up messages which are rather distressing, especially when I am standing there screening my calls, and which of course have spawned a whole host of *new* technological nonnecessities such as call answering and caller ID and *69, with Nynex calling me one day (the woman calling did, in fact, say: "This is Nynex calling") and offering a free phone to "preferred customers" to test their new built-in specialty service telephone (my only question is whether "preferred customer" means someone who uses the phone a lot, to which the Nynex woman replies that in fact, no, it doesn't, it simply means someone who pays their bills on time). I figure at the very least these trial-offered services may come in handy tracking down the wrong-number complete strangers who call and, seeing an occasion for Great Performance Art, launch into bizarre messages, like the woman who calls and says: "You creature, you little ass, you little bastard, gonna go over there and rape you. Bye," or the other woman who calls and says: "Don't you ignore me. If you ever ignore me like that again I will *smack your face*."

The phone answering machine debacle is even worse

where my family is concerned, since my parents are of the generation that still believes in dealing with things face to face (or, at the very least, ear to ear), unlike people my age who see nothing wrong with leaving twenty-minute messages on my machine as if I am sitting there captively listening to their one-sided missives *which of course I am*. The only thing wrong with my parents' approach is that it causes them to leave disturbingly cryptic messages like: "Dan, please call as soon as possible" or my favorite: "Dan, it's nothing to worry about, but please call when you get a chance" in voices reminiscent of in-shock hostages forced to say that all is well, or of William S. Burroughs if he were to have done that Channel 5 do-you-know-where-your-children-are? public service announcement that has made my flesh creep since the age of eight. To prevent me from worrying so much they now withhold information from me entirely, so secondhand and post facto I'll hear from my sister: "Did Mom tell you she broke her arm?" forcing me to obsess about *not* hearing from my parents, so much so that when my brother Jimmy calls from his girlfriend's house wondering if Mom called me today, since she left a message that something "serious" had happened, I look at my nonblinking answering machine and answer no while simultaneously going into High Anxiety Overdrive.

Jimmy shares my worry and asks if I can call my other brother, Ian, which I do, and Ian informs me that he hasn't heard anything either; I call my parents' house again just to double-check and I am greatly surprised when my mother answers, herself bewildered by my wondering if "everything is okay," and I explain that Jimmy called upset that something "serious" had happened and he couldn't get an answer at the house, and my mom informs me that they've been there all day but out in the backyard, and that the man who's writing a letter of recommendation for Jimmy called and needs to get a hold of him and that is *all*. I exasperatedly start in with my anti-cryptic-phone-messages soliloquy, my mom defensively recounts that her actual wording was "important" and not "serious," as call-waiting kicks in on my mother's line and I hang up just as my brother calls me back to explain that his girlfriend took the message that "it is important that Jimmy call home," to which she added "she sounds serious"—as in an actual game of telephone the phone message has gotten all jumbled up in the translation—and we convince ourselves that our own parents will give us heart attacks long before they themselves are in their graves, and I call back my brother Ian, who is furious since when he finally just got through to Mom she immediately started yelling at him: *"I didn't say it was SERIOUS; I said it was IMPOR-TANT!"* before he even got two words out of his mouth, at which point we decide that it might be useful to provide all the members of the family with beepers only to be used in case of *dire emergencies*.

The acute irony of technology speeding up the pace of life to the point that New Yorkers prefer to stay inside and communicate via phone or fax or online service as opposed to venturing out and meeting up with those same people *in real life* is not lost on me, hosting as I do some conferences on a New York–based bulletin board service and running an adjunctive Web site for my zine, all the while futilely attempting to completely break myself of my reliance on the so-called Internet, choosing to respond to e-mail by phone or in person instead of knee-jerkingly replying "instantaneously" by e-mail, since evoking emotion, or mood, or laughter, or anger via the computer-keyboarded word is a pretty silly state of affairs when you come right down to it. A huge portion of my time is spent answering the daily influx of e-mail I receive in response to my weekly diatribe about *Beverly Hills 90210*, which is posted every week to the vast knowledge wasteland that is the World Wide Web, and about which I receive six basic types of mail, numbering in the dozens of messages each day: friendly missives addressing me *personally* (Dear Danny), which I readily admit I enjoy getting; mail addressing me as *the show itself* (Dear 90210) and asking for an autographed picture of the entire cast or demanding to know why I let Dylan leave the show or wanting to know about a particular setting for a wedding or a particular song's origination and usually signed "Your biggest fan"; mail addressing me as a *character* on the show (Dear Donna, Dear Brandon) and asking for an autographed picture or at least a response usually with advice as to the character's future personal problem resolution; mail addressing me as an *actor portraying a character* on the show (Dear Jennie, Dear Brian) and asking for an autographed picture or some other reference material usually for personal-haircut purposes; mail berating *me impersonally* (To Whom It May Concern) for my misuse of punctuation, and of paragraphs, and of spelling, and of grammar, and of the English language as concerns regionalisms and dialects, and of the English language in its entirety, and of the English language to discuss anything perceived to be outside the scope of simply summarizing the show, which, since they perceive this to be my *job*, could I please just stick to that and nothing else as I have *customers to please*—reflecting in no small way a certain Internet-induced mindset of people who themselves use their work-provided technology not to do any actual *work*, but to inflict their narrow conformist sense of deserved service on a world now imperiled by their very virtual and frighteningly far-reaching presence.

In actuality, my plan to give up technology does not involve the actual smashing to bits of computer monitors or retiring to Amish country; I simply have stopped advancing with it, choosing to not need the biggest, fastest, newest, bestest; I'm perfectly content with my college-bought receiver and turntable and vinyl records; I'm used to the static world of my decade-old computer hardware and software; I actually prefer to not own an automobile, which is not stigmatizing only in New York City (I often think of the surreal beauty of Amsterdam Avenue during a snowstorm when there are no cars in sight whatsoever); and I imagine eventually, as my cherished old tech gives out, I will make up a new category outside of the technology haves and have-nots: the *had-but-don't-want-anymores*.

The Subway

The New York City Police Department has changed its policy of arresting all subway fare beaters, Police Commissioner William J. Bratton said yesterday. Mr. Bratton said that the objective of the original fare-beating sweeps by the police—imprisoning offenders found to be professional criminals or scofflaws with outstanding warrants—would continue. . . .

The policy change was first reported yesterday in The Daily News, which said it came as a result of the embarrassing arrests of Brian H. Moody, a Wall Street Journal circulation executive, and his mother, Mary. The two were put in handcuffs, fingerprinted and jailed for a night in June before charges of fare beating were dropped.

—The New York Times, *December 6, 1995*

I have always been amazed by the New York City subway system, even in the days of run-down graffitied trains, which I thought were much more worthwhile aesthetically speaking than half the current bodies of work posing as art in so-called art galleries in SoHo and back rooms of museums, which aren't free or public but which are "legal," but most of all after growing up in the Car Culture state of New Jersey, where walking home from the bus station or otherwise walking any distance over two miles through the streets of my hometown is considered a Highly Suspicious Activity, only slightly below that of using public transportation. The ancient underground world of our transit system is even more incredible when compared to the newer systems of other cities, like Los Angeles's system, which consists of some extremely expensive underground tunnels with no actual trains in most of them making for a rather warped ratio of means of conveyance to people actually conveyed, unless you consider those rainwater sluices that sweep people away on a regular basis as some strange form of mass transit; or that of Palo Alto, where my friend Sally tells me there isn't so much a train station as a slab of concrete where I can wait for the CalTrain to take me back to San Francisco on what is basically the Losers-without-Cars Express; or that of San Francisco, which despite its BART, and MUNI, and quaint cable cars, nonetheless has a focus on the automobile that puts New Jersey to shame, as was made vividly clear to me after I drove cross-country with my friend Laurel and went to replace her old knobbed car door lock buttons with the un-hanger-open-up-able kind at the "auto store," a huge depot-like affair dedicated to All Things Auto, with not only a whole section devoted to *car interiors* but a whole aisle devoted to *car door lock buttons* broken down by make and model, including the car door lock buttons for Laurel's twenty-year-old Plymouth Valiant, itself now roaming the highways of the Bay Area alongside gas-guzzling Land Rovers driven around by the multiple-vehicle-owning population with environmental activism bumperstickers sardonically plastered on every single last car they own.

Granted, despite the fact that riding the subway with half the city population every single day can be a unifying experience, commuting via subway in New York can also be quite hellish, especially when the temperature underground is twenty degrees hotter than the ninety-plus temperature outside; or when I calmly and resignedly slide down against a train door in a crowded subway car when I hear someone scream: "He's got a gun!" since there is *nowhere else to go*; or when the red drops I am following up the stairs that I hope are from some kid's cherry ice pop, but which I know deep down are drops of blood, manage to appear in front of me as I go through the turnstile, up the stairs to street level, and down the sidewalk as I head home as well, until I'm convinced that they are waiting to see which way I'm headed before appearing, in some twisted teleological-deterministic way; or the fire-and-brimstone preacher who stares at us while delivering his condemnation of homosexuals without mentioning the word *homosexuality*, recalling a preacher in San Francisco whom my friend Laurel and I listened to raptly for a full twenty minutes while waiting for a bus trying to understand why men should not be "humongous" when the correct term was in fact *whoremongers*. Likewise our Downtown Local Preacher is giving us a condemnation of "those lying with man as woman" and other confusing half-references to biblical passages of dubious translation into his particular brand of English, and I am content to simply frown at him until it hits me that the entire subway car is staring at *us* either with complete contempt or with anticipation of our reaction, with the self-anointed preacher not as bothersome as feeling like a coward *above and beyond* my perceived judgment at the hand of an entire subway car, and to prove some point or other I put my arm around the boyfriend, which doesn't seem to register with the preacher man but which does get a few smiles out of the assembled congregation.

In strictly Dante-esque terms, the subway is always one hell level closer to Abyss Central than anything that happens on the streets of the city. For this reason the subway should never be used as a refuge, or a destination in and of itself, since things only get worse once you descend those stairs into the city's very bowels;

I recall this rule after walking around town with my friend Shannon, who, with her equivalent but differently focused neuroses, complements me rather well. We are walking somewhat aimlessly since we both have the day off, ending up on Bleecker Street to impulse-shop a little bit, resulting in a brand-new annoyingly pink pigskin bag for me which I'm not sure I like ten minutes later, and then on another impulse buying Halloween candy by the bagful, which we definitely regret about a half hour later after we've consumed every last candy corn, and circus peanut, and cinnamon red-hot. Ambling up Fifth Avenue, we spy a girl that we knew from back in school who spots us and waves from across the street; we wave back with big smiles all the while telling each other that we hope she won't cross the street to come talk to us. Seeing her sets us off on a discussion of other people we knew back in school who we would likewise pray would not cross the street to come talk to us, when suddenly we see right in front of us one of the people we were just talking about not five minutes before; just as she is about to say hi, we simultaneously turn to each other and mouths agape both gasp aloud, seemingly doomed to run into everyone we ever knew and never wanted to see again in that particular small-world way New York has of haunting us past acquaintance–wise.

We decide to retreat to the subway so as to avoid any further unplanned meetings with people from our mutual past on the street; we sit down on an empty bench and wait for the train next to a rather grubby man leaning against a column who is just staring at us. Not innocuously, but rather boldly and unabashedly he gazes at us, unnerving us both no end as I try to stare back, my half-mustered false bravado no match for his unwavering eyes; I stare for two minutes or so, not a long time for him, I imagine, since he doesn't even wince, but an unending eternity for me; he wins, still glaring; I avert my gaze. By this point Shannon and I have worked ourselves up into a minor frenzy; we refuse to walk away, halfway out of fear that he will follow us. As the train pulls in I can't take it anymore, and pooling all my willpower together, I stand up and demand: "What the hell are you *staring at*?" Still staring hatefully, he pauses, then replies with a thick gurgly accent: "Faces. *Ug-ly* faces." We shut up, sit down, and wait for the next train.

Now, of course, the subways are cleaned up and the

stations are redone and the token is soon to be a thing of the past and efforts are made to combat crime in the subway and a lot of other bureaucratic make-the-subway-better decrees are being handed down, all of which I think absolutely not at all about in my daily journeys on New York City mass transit, instead focusing on my daily unvarying routine of get the paper/get a bagel/get on the subway/get to work. My particular morning journey involves walking down to 86th Street, where I buy my newspapers, and then to the post office on 83rd Street, where I check my box for mail, and then to the bagel shop at 81st Street to get my salt bagels and cream cheese or else my salt bagels and Sally Sherman's chopped egg salad; and when the line for bagels is long it means I'll be late to work, which puts me in a bad mood if I'm not already in a bad mood for not having any mail in my post office box as I then head to the 79th Street subway station a few blocks down from there.

If there is any subway skill that I have honed while living in this city it is the ability to immediately and without second thought reconfigure my subway trek to work; I have more alternate routes plotted out in my mind than the best civil defense organization in the world because there is invariably a problem that calls for split-second decision making on a par with that happening in governmental war rooms. The Seventh Avenue IRT local downtown to Seventh Avenue and 50th Street station is my Normal Route, which involves boarding and getting off a train only once, but which still leaves me with a long walk across town; my alternate route is the Seventh Avenue IRT express downtown to Times Square, and then the shuttle across to Grand Central, and then the Lexington Avenue IRT local up one stop, which brings me closer to my destination, but which comprises getting on and off three trains, thereby multiplying my chances of running into problems, the biggest of which is my unwilling participation in IRT Local Roulette, when the conductor without warning announces: "This train is now EXPRESS—next stop, Forty-second Street!" because they usually say it after we pass the express stop of 72nd Street, requiring the abovementioned reconfiguration of the original subway trek plans to work, which are now totally thrown to the wayside, leaving me late, cranky, and despising humanity in general and train dispatchers more specifically.

Some mornings start worse and only get worser, as I

get to the newsstand and they are sold out of newspapers and I get to the post office and there is no mail for me and I get to the bagel shop and the line is ridiculously long so I get no bagel and I have no token on me and the same homeless guy who is outside the store every day is collecting change and I have no change to give him as I go down into the subway station, which, being a local station, has only one small token booth and one token clerk to serve one of the more populous parts of the city. I queue up with a five-dollar bill in hand, only the token booth clerk is not in her booth but is calmly and very slowly collecting tokens from the turnstiles. As most New Yorkers can relate, this is a Typical Existential Moment that proves once again how we are unequivo-cably slaves to the transit system; I can't get over the insolence of this token clerk, dawdling and generally taking her time outside the protection of her booth in front of ten angry people waiting to buy tokens, as we stare at her and do that shared-moment looking at each other with can-you-top-this looks on our faces while train number one comes into the station and moves on.

Exasperated, we don't dare say anything; we are com-pletely at her mercy, as she must know. Train number two pulls in and leaves, and the subway part of my brain starts to calculate where the first train would be by this time, and where I would be on my journey if I had been on that train; this particular calculate-into-the-future feature of my brain usually prevents me from detraining a local to go express, since I know fatalistically no express train will arrive, while I will be tormented by the knowledge of how I would have been home by now if I had only stayed put. A third train rumblingly announces its approach. One of the guys in line with whom I've been sharing outraged glances this whole time looks at me. In a symbiotic I-will-if-you-will moment of understanding we both leave the line still clutching our money in our hands, and in a burst of adrenaline we jump over the turnstiles and sprint for the opening doors of the incoming train. Impeding our respective beelines are two men walking toward us; my heart races a mile a minute, the train is now home base, and a man is in my way, like in a surreal dream where something is just out of reach and as hard as I try I can't get to it; I sense that something is terribly wrong, which is proved true when the man blocking my way grabs my arm, flashes a badge, and tells me I'm under arrest.

In the backwards-in-time aspect of my above-mentioned brain capacity I often have the subway experience when I miss a train of backtracking and plotting out how if I had left home earlier, or if I had not bought the newspaper, or if I had not done any other thing, I would no doubt be on that train right now. As I am pulled to the side of the platform I retreat into the near past: if only I had gone somewhere else to get the paper, which I had not; and if only I hadn't gone to check my mail, which I had; and if only I had stopped and bought a bagel, which I had not; and if such regrets were dollar bills I'd be a pretty rich man by now. The plain-clothed policemen tell us to put our arms behind our backs as we are painfully handcuffed, driving home that this is, in fact, happening to me, like some toned down low budget version of *Midnight Express*. Before he searches me the policeman asks me if I have any drugs, or weapons, or syringes in my pocket that might stick him, and I roll my eyes—thinking, Don't get excited; this is going to be the most banal *Cops* show of your entire career—but I only say no. As he goes through my pockets he finds a dry cleaning receipt, and a gum wrapper, and there, amidst some dollar bills and lint and store receipts is: a token.

I backtrack wildly in my mind to an imaginary what-if point in the recent past that has me finding the token in my pocket, happily boarding the train, and merrily going off to work; but the resulting if-onlys reach a kind of critical mass of resignation, at which point I just give up. I ask the smirking cop: "You found five dollars in my hand, why would I have five dollars in my hand?" which only ends up sounding utterly incriminating. We are moved into a broom closet of a tiny room that acts as a vantage point for sweep-happy surveilling transit cops to spy on the subway station. A guy who in the old days would have been called a bum on the Bowery but today is domiciledly disadvantaged is asleep and reeking of bad whiskey on the bench we are seated on as they bombard us: "Why did you do it?" "Are you guys in this together?" "Where were you headed?" "Were you going together?" The sounds of their voices are distant as I concentrate on my inability to relax my face muscles since every expression feels confrontational somehow; I want to say, "Yeah, I'm playing Bonnie in this huge fare-beating racket I've got going with Clyde here," but I tell the truth, if only to deny the implied conspiracy, although I feel like I'm explaining to my mom that I took money out of her purse to buy her a present—I *still* did something wrong.

They put my "affairs" (including my NYU keychain, which I bought because I saw it while exiting the NYU bookstore one day and I needed a keychain—there is no love lost between me and NYU, to which I have mortgaged my future) into an envelope, and the cop who had previously asked us where we were going to which the other "perp" responded, "To take my Culinary Institute exams upstate" now says, "We got ourselves a couple of scholars here!" He asks me what I learned in that "liberal-run institution." Then he asks us for whom we voted in the last election. Then he picks up *The New York Times* and says, "Let's see what the liberals had to say today," and I want to say, "I'll take Conservative Guideposts for a thousand dollars, Alex"—but I don't.

The unfolding drama is ridiculous in an unnecessarily defensive confrontational way, and I realize the Bad Idea it would be to bring up my general revulsion in watching those *Cops* cops who subvert the Fourth, Fifth, Sixth, and Eighth Amendments to the Constitution on a regular basis; or how I feel that cops should live in the neighborhoods they serve, which might prevent them from talking about "project pussy" to the housing cop making an appearance just now. My co-perp, on the other hand, now missing his final exams, makes small talk with the policemen, asking them about the sweep logistics and perp statistics and other topics of major inanity; his behavior disgusts me, since I know that rats like him who cozy up to the screws are reviled in the Big House. I ask to make a phone call in a this-is-a-TV-moment way, only I have to wait until we arrive at the station house since they have one more quota-filling farebeater to snag.

"Nice snare you set up with the token clerk" the other guy says, in a lame attempt at perp humor; it rankles the cops and is exactly what I'm thinking, but I'm glad I'm not the one who says it.

The drunk guy awakes and asks to have his handcuffs loosened, requiring an agonizing repositioning on our part while they make him comfortable at our expense, and on closer inspection he doesn't look so much like a bum as much as Michael Caine on a really bad day, although a bit too proud for someone in his shoes, as he lectures us—literally a captive audience—on proper post-arrest pre-jail behavior. We torturously listen for the arrival of each train, hoping in despicable war-movie style for the capture of someone else from our side. When the fourth farebeater turns out to be a crackhead, I sigh in relief, since he isn't someone I might feel embarrassed in front of or, worse, someone I know from the neighborhood. The cops escort us out of the subway into waiting police cars, 59th Street–Columbus Circle subway stationhouse bound, as the culinary school guy and I sit quietly in the backseat. I try to make conversation; I echo his earlier remark about the setup and wonder if he is going to flunk out. His curt answers bother me, since they lead me to believe that perhaps he is not giving me the benefit of the doubt that I am not a scumbag or worse, which I find absolutely appalling. The cop up front turns and looks at us and I can't cop-show-wise recall if backseat prisoner convo is allowed or not, so I stop, not wanting to be the Jack Nicholson in *One Flew over the Cuckoo's Nest* troublemaker, when in fact he is only telling us that we've reached Columbus Circle. We enter the dank dark booking room, take off our shoelaces and belts suicide-prevention style, and are put behind bars, where I look at my comrades-in-jail observing me right back in my shirt-and-tie work clothes and I try to maintain an air of homicide or worse so that they leave me alone. Meanwhile, arising around me is a litany of complaints and excuses and the modern equivalent of Edward G. Robinsonian "I was framed, see?" un-incrimination antics entirely lost not only on the couldn't-care-less New York cops, but on the inmates sharing the in-jail circumstance with those protesting their innocence.

I don't understand the juvenile part of the human psyche that makes up lies and delusions to justify wrong-doing, similar to a child who steals something, or breaks something, or lies to somebody and then is caught in that theft, or vandalism, or falsehood and ends up not just simply denying it, but *loudly and exaggeratedly* denying it, only compounding the child's guilt; it may be that the first time a child lies to its parents at the age of two and they *believe* him he feels a certain subconscious exhilaration at the revelation that it is possible to lie and get away with it, but this still goes only a short way in revealing why my cell mate, obviously a bike messenger, who with his helmet and padding looks like what humans might look like today if they had evolved from cockroaches and not apes, feels the need to protest loudly: "Look, I'm delivering a package! It's *important*!"

The cop's surly response is: "You know what? We get fifty of you messengers in here every day, fifty of you at a hundred bucks a pop; scumbags like you pay my salary!" It hits me at that moment that in New York—the financial capital of the world—billions of dollars in transactions and contracts and business deals at any given point in time are being sped around the city on the backs of reckless messengers under pressure job-wise to break the law, and I imagine the revolution that would take place if messengers simply *stopped delivering*.

Another guy persistently asks if he "can go now," ignoring the iron bars and padlocks that make it obvious that it isn't really an option to leave just yet. It dawns on me that the antisuicide measures are not to keep us from killing ourselves because we're ashamed of what we've done, but from killing ourselves because we have to listen to the unending appeals for release from detainees obviously *not going anywhere fast*. The detectives have also tired of the asylum seeker and run his background check, and finding a list of outstanding warrants and a record a mile long, inform him that he "can go now," only meaning downtown to Central Booking and then extradited back to the state his warrants are from. As he is led out, I look around and try to imagine what other *America's Most Wanted* warrants await discovery on the rest of the rabble stuck in jail with me, but soon stop, on the verge of a self-induced nervous breakdown.

"DRENNAN! You wanted to make a phone call?"

The cop's booming doing-me-a-favor voice startles me and nearly sends me over the edge; I entertain the notion of never going back to work at all and what that might mean career-wise. The phone I use to call my boss is right next to a detective at his desk, who gives me no privacy and a dirty look; my boss answers the phone and as cheerfully as I am able I say: "I had a bit of a problem this morning and am going to be late for work today," and when my boss asks me if anything is wrong I add: "Well, I am kind of . . . in jail," which is followed by an interminable silence made only slightly less uncomfortable by my joking attempt to make light of what happened: "It's a long story, but I was late and I jumped a turnstile and I got arrested—" at which point the detective next to me yells much louder than is absolutely necessary: "What the FUCK do you think this is? A FUCKING hotel? *Get the FUCK off the phone!*"

Another long pause.

"Um, I guess you have to go," my boss offers, and I hang up and return, chastised, to the jail cell. The cop who originally arrested me says: "What did you tell him?" and I answer with: "The truth," which seems to impress the guy, as the truth is perhaps an anomaly in the New York City justice system, and it's like on *N.Y.P.D. Blue* when the hardened New York City cop shows his human side for one split second.

The processing of my case begins with someone snapping my Polaroid, and some rookie cop who won't look anybody in the eye taking my fingerprints; and I have to stand there, a little bit over here, now turn a little, now present your arm, now turn, okay now palm down and fingers extended, basically doing a little dance with the rookie cop who is all the time holding my hand in some bizarre hoedown only minus the fiddle music; I almost start laughing, wanting to make a joke about having this dance, and when he finishes I preposterously feel obliged to thank him. I wash my hands and get my things; I grab my coat, and my bag, and my belt, and my shoelaces, and the envelope with my personal belongings just like in those prison movies, and they give me a paper with the date of my court appearance and tell me I can't lace up my shoes in the station house, practically ejecting me bodily laces in hand into the subway again where I pretend to tie my shoelaces when in reality I am lacing them up from scratch; and I stand there, four hours after leaving for the subway that morning and back in the subway again, about to board the Number 9 train for home and still nowhere near work, feeling that it is somehow evident that I was just in jail, that either my countenance has changed, or my appearance is a giveaway that I was just ten minutes before locked up in a jail cell in the hidden depths of the New York City subway system.

I do not in the least feel liberated or relieved even though nothing I am doing is out of the ordinary; I am taking the subway home where I am going to wash up and walk the dog and go back to work where everyone is expecting me; I am walking and moving and carrying on my life like every other normal person I pass on my way home, yet in my head I am dealing with the fact that I just spent five hours getting arrested and going to jail; I feel as though I am expected to continue my normal life even though in the past five hours I've been arrested, in jail, photographed, fingerprinted, and released; and even stranger is the sensation that as long as I don't talk about it to anyone else, then *somehow it didn't happen.*

At work everyone is supportive, although for all they know I jump the turnstile each and every day and just happened to get caught this one time, and they listen to me call the boyfriend and some other friends with my only recourse being to make light of the excruciatingly dismal day I've had: "Oh yeah, got arrested, went to jail, ha ha." Someone decides to take Polaroid mug shots of me as a little joke, not at all aware as I feebly play along that it makes me sick to my stomach. When I get home later, I call my father since he went to law school for a while and might have some post-ordeal what-to-expect advice. He consults with his best-friend-since-forever Brooklyn-based lawyer-buddy, who listens to my father telling him my story, punctuating every other word "okay, okay, okay" until he gets to the part about the cop finding a token on me, at which point our lawyer says: "He found a token in his pocket? Forget about it! He's dead. Dead! Tell him to pay his fine and get the hell out of there!"

I am a bit taken aback by my so-called on-my-side lawyer throwing me to the lions so mercilessly, but I resign myself to my day in court and my lack of choice and my eventual fine and my splitting headache and I sit on the couch for the rest of the evening in a bit of a dazed stupor, until the boyfriend comes home, when I break down and sob hysterically for close to an hour.

A month later my day in court arrives; working freelance as I am, losing a day of work to my court date is already more than I can afford before we even get to the monetary fine calculation of this criminal equation. I find the courtroom, where entrance is limited to those with a case number, like an exclusive nightclub that only caters to alleged criminals, in an old dingy New York City court building that has remained unchanged since time immemorial. Someone announces that court will start promptly at nine; someone else halfheartedly bellows: "Please rise!" announcing the presiding Honorable Judge by name, and here comes the judge, shuffling into the chamber with his robe undone, schlepping a bagel, a coffee, a newspaper, and generally going against every image I've ever had in my head of judge-like behavior. Without acknowledging anyone he sits on his bench and reads the paper while eating his bagel and drinking his coffee, quite impressively letting me down with his dishonorable pomp-and-circumstancelessness.

The cases are presented one by one, with waiting cases called out to the rotunda outside the courtroom. This is where I meet my public defender when it's my turn; she gives me her cruddy white heavy-stock-paper business card with her name and the words "Public Defender" underneath, perfectly summing up her thankless no-glamour non-dream-team job, and I describe the scenario behind my case while feeling that creeping sense of guilt that comes with trying to seem not guilty. She points out the community-service-sentencing leanings of this judge, as I ask pleadingly, "Okay, but can't I just pay a fine or something?" since I prepared myself based on my father and my father's lawyer's advice, the judge's no-fine attitude representing a huge wrench in the works. I tell her about the pro bono work I do for a local crime prevention organization, as well as my volunteer role as a drug watcher on my block, which was true enough since I was always on my phone calling the Crack Hotline from the comfort of my home at the window behind a curtain, although of course I edit out the homemade weaponry part of the story, trying beyond hope to convince her that all of this might somehow be considered "community service" since I can't afford to lose another day of work, and that I simply want to pay my fine and then go home.

She suggests to my great alarm that any such request will result in double the community service along with a fine as we reenter the courtroom and present ourselves in front of the judge who doesn't look at me but asks how I plead.

"Guilty, your honor."

The absence of mitigating circumstance, or a trailing "but," or the chance to explain is extraordinarily strange to me, with the whole concept of justice rendered irrevocably fluid and meaningless as I realize that jumping a turnstile, which set off a whole chain of events that were in no way proportional to or reflective of the original crime, has wound down into this one clear-cut moment, which is equally in no way reflective of or proportional to the original crime as I pronounce the words "Guilty, your honor" to the judge, who sentences me to community service and warns me that if I violate the conditions of my community service my case will be restored on the court calendar and a warrant will be issued for my arrest subjecting me to full prosecution on the original charges and that if I successfully complete my service the charges would be dropped and my records sealed. The bailiff gives me my stamped and signed paper and sends me upstairs, where sitting in an empty hallway is a woman at a small desk with a stack of papers in front of her, whom I do not assume at all to be officiating, but that is exactly what she is doing at a desk in the middle of the corridor. She without pause tells me that I have been accepted into the Transit Police Department's Community Service Program, that I will give one day of my time toward the improvement of the Transit Authority System; she gives me yet another piece of paper, which is my work detail assignment, and I go home after another day spent caught up in the gummy machinery of a legal system in which nothing actually ever gets accomplished but the wheels and cogs and gears inexorably turn and turn and turn.

A month later, I'm down in the subway on my way to the subway station where I will do my subway time for my subway crime, and I don't know if there is anything worse than taking the subway somewhere at eight o'clock on a Saturday morning except perhaps having to be at the Grand Central Station terminus for the S shuttle at eight o'clock on a Saturday morning to report for my community service, where I find a mass of teenage boys just hanging, with not a one talking or otherwise making any sound, and who are, in fact, on a long winding line of a hundred or so kids basically half my age that I join, finding myself to my great embarrassment the oldest misdemeanorer in the whole place. They take us in groups of ten, check our papers, check off our names, and send our group off with our supervisor to the Number 4 train to Mosholu Parkway station at 206th Street in the Norwood section of the Bronx, a great relief to me, fearing a 96th Street station detail that would have me running into someone I know.

We are handed off by the supervisor to the station janitor, who plies us with brooms, and bleach, and hoses, and instructions on how to hose down the subway station, and it is like that part of "The Walrus and the Carpenter" from *Through the Looking Glass* where the two antagonists ponder whether "seven maids with seven mops" sweeping a beach for half a year could clear it of sand, since we could have spent eternity cleaning that subway station and it would be no cleaner—proved true when we set to work with our hoses and brooms and bleach and the dirt of a hundred years comes pouring by in fetid black rivulets. One of the boys refuses to work at all, another catcalls women coming into the station; I sense the concept of punishment is lost on them and the only real remorse felt is for having been *caught*. At our lunch break we go to the corner bodega and eat in the drizzle until someone breaks the posturing silence to ask what we are all in for, whereupon we enumerate our petty crimes: tagging the subway, spray-painting graffiti along a highway, and my crime, jumping a turnstile, which I announce sotto voce, half expecting derisive laughter but receiving only a knowing "I've been in for that before" from some guy half my age, already progressed beyond my criminal specialty. Another guy says, in all serious-ness, "You know, that janitor, he makes about fifty grand a year!" followed by: "My friend Revs says they pay tag-gers nine bucks an hour to paint lampposts silver."

I'm shocked; everyone in New York knows that "Revs" and his nemesis "Cost" are two of the most virulent and infamous taggers in the city, having blanketed the entire cityscape with wheat-pasted leaflets reading COST and REVS and other assorted messages pertaining to each other, and whereas Revs is out scot-free making a name for himself and basically attaining famousness for papering inch by inch all the walled surfaces of New York City, this kid is doing time, looking forward to a just-above-minimum-wage Sisyphean job silver-painting over REVS signs on lampposts. He continues, explaining how he's run away from home twice and is about to drop out of school as I just listen since there's not much more I can do, although sometimes I think listening at the time might have been enough. He suddenly turns and abruptly asks me point blank: "Yo, man, how old are you?" Startled, I manage to throw the ball back in his court with: "How old do you *think* I am?" He pauses and replies: "Twenty-three or something?" and I start to laugh because he has no idea how much he's made my day. I finally say: "No, I'm thirty," which he can't quite get over, though I don't push my luck and ask why not.

For two more hours we sweep, and mop, and clean, and we're left covered in muck and dirt, our clothes bleached out. When the supervisor informs us that our detail is done we all catch the downtown train, the other boys Brooklyn-bound, and all of us making a sorry sight in our filthy clothes reeking of chlorine; they seem to take it better than I do, and, as I get off at 96th Street, feeling completely tired and demoralized and only looking forward to a long hot shower before sleeping the rest of the day, I somewhat-seriously say: "Stay out of trouble guys!" as their laughter echoes in my head, the Revs boy already busy at work tagging the aluminum doors with a piece of broken glass.

The Neighborhood

If someone with Tourette's syndrome moves to New York City, can they still be classified as having the disorder?

New Yorkers, contrary to their reputation for being cold and uncaring, are quite the opposite: behind the shields erected to protect their personal space are individuals facing the paradox of being alone among millions of people. The result is a city of people quick to open up and reach out—usually for the better, sometimes for the worse. I run into many of these people on a daily basis, be they neighbors, or street people, or merchants, or the guy walking his dog who insists on talking to me while politely asking his Weimeraner to be "Mister Manners," or the blind woman smacking my leg with her cane at the corner of 96th Street and Broadway and screaming at me: *"Hey! why don't you watch where you're walking!"*

Sometimes I simply observe, usually during my walks with Czaro down by the rebuilt seawall along the Hudson River where people now go once again to be reminded that they actually live on an *island*, watching the people whose oddball day-in-and-day-out behavior fascinates me and becomes less oddball in the long run since, in fact, they are no different from me as I walk my dog and also do the same thing day in and day out. The cast of characters in this real-life theater-in-the-round meanders about the park, their various roles never played the same way twice, but their mannerisms making them instantly recognizable: there is the decked-out-in-ocular-paraphernalia man who, weighed down by tons of binoculars, video cameras, regular cameras, and telephoto lenses—some of which measure three feet long—listens for planes and helicopters and then, gyrating wildly to corroborate aural sensory input with visual, slings around his nocs or camera or video camera in quick succession once he has a lock on the target. I get tired just looking at the fifty-odd pounds of equipment that he carries around with him, including a little computer he has, into which he sometimes enters data, or out of which he sometimes swaps little diskettes. I imagine him to be some sort of planespotter, and I'm reminded of my father's stories from his boyhood about the identifying marks of U-boats and German planes people were supposed to look for when the Nazis finally invaded the East Coast during World War II; like the fabled Japanese soldiers abandoned on forgotten outer-Pacific atolls, perhaps this man has never been informed that the war is actually *over*.

There is the woman in Riverside Park who walks around bent over looking at weeds—poking, prodding, picking weeds, looking at them, and then *eating* them—and who makes a ponderous face as she chews, as if wondering whether that is the weed she *thinks* it is. I think perhaps this is one of the authors of the book about identifying and harvesting edible and medicinal plants, whose coauthor was arrested for eating dandelions in Central Park. The book contains such choice tips as "there are highly poisonous members of the legume family that can cause paralysis and death," and gives not-so-helpful recommendations for differentiating the right sumac for a hollandaise sauce recipe from the poisonous variety, the toxin of which "[causes] a painful rash [that] can last for weeks, spreading all over your body." I stand transfixed as I watch her risky weedeater behavior, slightly worried that sudden paroxysms of imminent death might interrupt her nettle-some chow-down at any instant.

There is also the woman I call the Poetry Lady, since she always carries around really skinny books, reciting verse aloud as she walks in the park. This performance, however, has a diametrically opposed counterpart as she goes from reading aloud to hiding behind trees—from no one in particular. The catch-22 is, of course, that since the people in the park walk by and studiously ignore her, they play into her idea that she's successfully hiding from everyone *in the first place*.

Some of the people I run into have some kind of beef with the world, or some religious or political motivation that impels them to make modern-day soapbox speeches in the public squares of New York that no longer exist for that purpose. I don't necessarily mean those guys in Times Square who claim to be the real Tribe of Israel but look more like the backup band for Parliament than ancient religious scholars, and who abuse all manner of passersby with their rapid-fire randomly read biblical passages; or the Antiabortion Bus parked a block away;

or the two women who man an antipornography table every once in a while and whom I once saw flee from Camille Paglia, who descended upon them Gatling-gun anti-anti-pornography style, drawing a much bigger crowd than they had to begin with. I much prefer the more subtle approach, like that of the man who usually stands at Broadway and 83rd Street, in no way bringing attention to himself in dress or manner except for the fact that he is berating at great length the people who walk by: "Break the stigma, people! Speak out in public!" His postmodern non-call-to-arms sums up the entire false world of passivism, that brand of don't-actually-do-anything antiactivism that entails wearing a ribbon, or buying some product because of its ersatz tie to charity, or supporting companies that wrap their consumerism in some feel-good karmic kickback scheme, or setting up ridiculously vapid publicity campaigns such as the Do Something organization, which once had a "Brick" award for best Dosomethinger whose Dosomethingness was some not-so-much-do-as-feel-good-for-talking-about activity; and if there could be an award for self-serving pointless PR campaigns I would like it to weigh fifty tons and to have it dropped from a ten-story building on the flat little head of the head of Do Something, Incorporated. My other favorite is the woman I usually see when I'm waiting for the crosstown M72 bus to the East Side, a one-woman rebuttal to the talk show she has tuned in on her earphone/radio combo with huge antenna; her running conversation with the program on the radio offers those around her a glimpse into what the subject of the program must be, and when the wait for the bus is long enough she breaks into rants about the Transit Authority that I am convinced correspond to the commercial breaks during the radio show. Instead of giving us dead silence during those commercial breaks she provides instead live antiadvertisements for New York City Public Transportation: "That bastard Giuliani, he crippled it! The buses don't run on time! All those cutbacks, and we still pay a dollar fifty," she cackles to no one and everyone, who give her a wide berth as she paces back and forth. Incredibly, after complaining for twenty minutes about the buses running late, she doesn't get on the bus that finally arrives, but even more astounding is the fact that despite the strange looks and cautious stares, those passengers now boarding are not talking about the ranting woman we left behind but about the fare increases, and the bad service on city buses. This woman—this town crier—stays behind, spreading her message to the masses.

There exists an entire group of people who fall into the category of Pedestrian Inhibitor, like those tourists leisurely strolling ten abreast who manage to keep me from maintaining my normal brisk walking clip; or the seasonal tchotchke sellers who block entire sidewalks with their counterfeit contraband; or the even more seasonal people descended from the forested parts of the North American continent like New Hampshire and Nova Scotia and Quebec who come to New York at Christmas and sell dead trees to already tree-starved New Yorkers, providing I imagine a definite twisted pleasure to such so-called close-to-nature folk as they sell expired pines and passed-on firs for ten bucks a foot to people who live in a concrete jungle.

Closer to home are neighbors and storeowners with whom I have actual conversations, like the guy on my block whose discussions are usually limited to his car and the weather, such that when I say: "Hi how are you," his pat reply is along the lines of: "Pretty cold out today!"

and when I try to cause trouble by asking: "Car won't start?" he answers defensively: "No! No! It's fine, just checking it for damage." I can't imagine what damage he's referring to, since, truth be told, I never see him *driving* the vehicle, but I think it might be weather-related. There is the doorman of the building next to mine who always tells me that I need a coat for my dog despite my protests that my dog can barely muster enough dignity as it is without silly dog clothes on; and the woman I see on occasion at the corner of Broadway tugging on people's jackets and asking them a question, with some of them shaking their heads no and some of them nodding their heads yes, and with those responding in the affirmative getting another earful from her along with a big smile before she moves on and starts tugging on someone else's coat, causing me to wonder what the question might be that she post-answer continues asking. As curious as I am I never seem able to time my arrival at the corner correctly to be the one questioned, which becomes a game of sorts, like walking quicker to catch a blinking WALK/DON'T WALK light, only in this case *hoping* to be stopped at the corner. My chance finally arrives while walking the dog as I get to the corner and wait for the light to change and the woman, bundled up in a full-length down-filled purple jacket and wraparound sunglasses, approaches me and pulls on my arm.

"You a *Jew*?" she asks abruptly.

"Excuse me?" I respond, surprised.

"You a *Jewwwww-uh*??" she repeats insistently, the "Jew" portion of the question verging on turning into a multisyllabic word the way she drags it out for my benefit.

Flustered by the strange request concerning my religious status as well as a bit defensive since it really is none of her business, I say, "No, *sorry*," since it seems very important to her, although it is offputting to hear myself apologizing for not being a certain religion as she, visibly perturbed by my non-Jewishness, turns sharply from me, grabs someone else's sleeve, and inquires again: "You a Jew?"

When I was young, my neighborhood was pretty evenly mixed Jews and Gentiles, though the difference wasn't made obvious to us in any way, and coming home from kindergarten one day I ran into an older kid who lived down the street, who I could tell had something to ask me by the look on his face.

"Are you Hanukkah or Christmas?"

I had never heard the word *Hanukkah* before and I couldn't process the question without a definition, but at that age I didn't know how to ask someone to be more precise, so I could only manage to ask, "What?"

"Are you Han-u-kkah—or are you Christ-mas??"

It sounded like an either/or question to me, but I couldn't imagine what the opposite of "Christmas" might be, so I asked, a bit frightened now, "What?"

He grabbed me, and started yelling in my face: "Are you candles or the tree?! *Candles,* or the *tree*?!"

"The *tree*! *THE TREE!*" I screamed, breaking free and running all the way home, crying my eyes out.

Standing at the corner, all I want to know is what the payoff is for the correct reply. "Yes," states the other woman; I wait for the jackpot.

The wraparound sunglasses lady leans in to her and lets go with a long drawn out guttural "Shaaaaaabbeeess!" which is, of course, short for *Guten Shabbes*, or "Good Shabbes," which means "Good Sabbath," and I feel left out, since I don't get a "Shabbes" from the seeming Shabbes Dispenser for this part of town.

Czaro meanwhile, perhaps realizing we won't actually

anytime soon arrive at nearby Joan of Arc Island park, takes about three steps and performs his little I'm-cold one-paw-up gesture; I pick him up and make my way home, stopping to buy a bottle of wine at the liquor store, where the rather toothless owner starts telling me yet again the story of how his wife's dog down in Puerto Rico looks exactly like mine except it is white and eats nothing but fried chicken; he then translates the story into Spanish for one of the cashiers, who I'm sure understood it perfectly fine in English the first time; this happens so often that I can basically say "my wife's dog down in Puerto Rico looks just like that only it is white and eats nothing but fried chicken" in Spanish. He is interrupted by a woman who comes into the store; I recognize her from *All My Children*, where her character had the year before been left behind by her soap-opera husband for another soap-opera lady, and I am not at all surprised to see her since I have at one time or another seen most everyone from *All My Children*'s Pine Valley in my neighborhood, like Tad Martin, and Joey Martin who I saw walking with Will Cortlandt, and Dimitri Marick walking up Broadway, and Brian Bodine, and Michael Delaney at a restaurant, and Miles Christopher in a café, and Brooke English at a movie premiere, and Jake Martin wearing gym clothes on 65th Street, and Anton Marick riding up on his bike to the theater where he was doing an off-Broadway play, which, I admit, I was going to see because he was in it; and on some level it is unusual for me to be familiar with fictional television town denizens for a much longer time than I've known some of my closest friends. The woman from *All My Children* is obviously upset and can't seem to make up her mind which kind of vodka she wants: "Um, yes, oh, I don't care, just give me THAT one," picking some bottom-shelf brew behind the counter as she starts to cry. The store owner stops and then states matter-of-factly: "I'm sorry Miss, I can't serve you, you are obviously inebriated and I will not serve you, thank you, good night," which might have been a gentlemanly thing to say if he didn't shout it out loud for the entire store to hear.

It becomes clear that the *All My Children* lady passed inebriated a long time ago; she is, in fact, tanked as she slurringly defends herself: "I just had a fight with my boyfriend, I'm a little upset that's all," compulsively brushing her hair out of her face while I imagine her boyfriend to be the character who left her television-drama-wise. The entire store is now watching the altercation as the owner stands firm: "I'm sorry Miss, I won't be serving you. Good night!" The *All My Children* lady's face flushes as she angrily replies, "Do you know who I am? I . . . am . . . an . . . *actress*!" the last word delivered about an octave higher than the rest of the statement, which only brings on the owner's final rebuttal: "I don't care if you're the *Pope*—I'm not serving you. Good night," as she starts crying again, gives a frustrated yell, and leaves the store, slamming the door behind her; my impulse is to run after her, telling her not to worry, that her soap-opera husband will eventually come back to her after he gets tired of that other soap-opera lady. I think better of it, buy my bottle of Brouilly instead, and head for home, walking past the Shabbes lady still dispensing, past the doorman who gives me a vindicated that-dog-needs-a-jacket look, past the guy still looking at his car who tells me: "Looks like snow!" and into the relative sanctuary of my building.

The Neighbors

We hold a tenant meeting to organize around some building-related problem that probably still exists but which I don't remember at all and which fills me with a great feeling of grass-roots activism and other idealistic notions of Us-versus-Them-ism; the only people who show up, however, are Complainers and Gossipers, both of whom ignore the more-pressing building problem to endlessly and untiringly complain and gossip about everyone who didn't show up at the meeting. Over the course of a boisterous two hours we manage to accomplish absolutely nothing, but I'm glad I show up, if only because I can't stand the idea of people talking about me behind my back.

My neighbors are an eclectic mix of people, from an older generation of escapees from war-ravaged Europe who moved here fifty years ago and whose combined life stories could fill books and books, to newer generations who've grown up in the building, including assorted artist types whose creative output pleasantly fills the lobby and halls with opera arias and piano recitals; and despite the fact that my friend Marjorie thinks at times we should just put bars on all the windows (including ours) and call it an institution, there is something rather comforting in knowing most everyone in my building, with certain holidays like Halloween finding more trick-or-treaters arriving at our doorstep for homemade peanut butter cookies in the so-called impersonal city than for the must-be-wrapped candy at my parents' home out in suburban New Jersey.

The demarcation line between outside world and inner sanctuary was first made clear by the sign that greeted us as we moved in, asking people in no uncertain terms not to let any strangers into the building; vigilante-in-the-making that I was, I was ready to do my share.

Later that first day in our new apartment, the buzzer sounds.

"Who is it?" I ask, not expecting anyone, and fumbling with the triple-buttoned new-to-me door buzzer.

"It's FAYE," comes the reply.

"I don't know who you are," I offer back, proudly doing my part to thwart this interloper.

"What do you *mean*, you don't know who I am? It's *FAYE!*" the voice chastens.

The voice is so insistent that I don't quite know what to do; no one has informed me about secret codes, or passwords, or special names to use, or people whose very existence overrides the security measures of the building, and so I buzz Faye in, and not hearing anything later that day about break-ins, or old-lady pharmacy-scam racketeering in the building, I relax a bit, though still not wanting to be the weak link in our new building's protective security chain.

Weeks turn into months as I daily perform my electronic doorman duties for the up-to-now unseen but quite heard Faye; until the fateful day when my dog-walking schedule and Faye's comings and goings intersect in the elevator, with Faye, unaware of who I am, completely ignoring me except to demand that I hold the door open as she shuffles inside. I'm surprised, since her commanding voice is contradicted directly by her actual presence: perhaps the oldest tenant in the building, Faye weighs all of next-to-nothing, has dyed jet-black hair held in place with quite Riot Grrrl–looking silver barrettes, and wears fashion ensembles that have seen a generation or two go by and have come full circle back in style. Faye *rocks*. Faye can barely see, and so she pounds on the buttons downstairs until she finds someone to let her in; with our button right next to the super's, we are second in line; but we're more than Faye's doormen, since running into Faye usually brings on a plea of "Can you help me out, doll?" as Faye savagely lords it over everyone in the building who become her serfs: holding doors open, buzzing her in, helping her up the stairs to the mailboxes.

Faye proudly announces to me one day that she was the "first illegitimate daughter" on the Upper West Side; another time she criticizes my laundry, explaining that she never does wash: "Off the body and into the sink!" she explains. Faye tells me sad stories about her dearly departed dog every time she sees me walking mine; sometimes I walk with her as she slowly, slowly makes her way around the block with one hand on the building at all times so as not to lose her way or her balance. Faye is age-defyingly active, going out a couple of times a day, which means that a couple of times a day I am called to the buzzer to be yelled at by Faye wanting to come inside, the tone of her voice never wavering in its insistence, no matter how many times I open the door for her. "It's FAYE!" she hollers.

Since the dog goes crazy every time the buzzer goes off it becomes instantly noticeable when Faye *doesn't* buzz up; the day that I stop hearing from Faye slowly goes by, with the appointed times of Faye's entrances coming and going with no sign of her whatsoever, leaving me worried yet chiding myself for even thinking about it in the first place. That afternoon the buzzer goes off and I happily go to answer the door.

"Hello—this is Faye's *son*," the garbled voice announces.

My immediate reaction is that a friend is playing a trick on me, or that I am not hearing quite right; I wonder, though, how Faye's son would know about me (maybe Faye told her son about me?); I wonder above all about the Upper West Side's first Love Child never mentioning anything about having a son in the first place. The voice pleads: "My mother is not answering her buzzer—can you let me in the building?" I buzz him in, and halfway want to run down to the third floor to see what happened, feeling slightly uneasy the rest of the day, since as distracting as the constant buzzing was, its silence is not-so-surprisingly worse.

I never do hear from Faye again, and I never did ask anyone what happened, not really wanting to know the answer but overhearing that she had to be taken to a rest home, where I imagine her shuffling around the corridors in her couture original polyester ensembles, leaning on her call button fifty times a day, creating general mayhem and panic among the other residents and staff. My only desire, when I finally reach the ripe old age of ninety, is to somehow be *half* the rampaging diva that Faye was.

I try to maintain this level of courtesy and helping out (not at all exemplified by our vitriolic so-called mayor and his incredibly hypocritical calls for city-wide politesse) that I imagine used to be a part of New York City life, which I hear in the way the older ladies of the building refer to each other as "Mrs. So-and-so" when speaking about mutual friends—an Old Worldism that just maybe can survive in one apartment building even if it has disappeared from the city at large. One of my regular tasks awaits me every Friday evening when a crowd forms outside the elevator, since it's Shabbes, and the more orthodox in my building are waiting for someone to open the elevator door; I find it reassuring that people raised in other faiths can grow up and still comfortably practice their religious beliefs, unlike recovering Catholics such as myself who instead worry about spontaneously combusting while attending someone's wedding or funeral or merely walking past St. Patrick's Cathedral. Usually people don't have to wait too long for someone to come by and open the elevator door and push the buttons for their destinations, except during Shabbes Rush Hour, just around sundown on Friday evening, or on the occasions when I come into my hall and the one-stop-shopping stamps-and-coupons lady from my building—who sells stamps at a markup and collects favors like a loan shark so she can later ask me if I won't go down to Delancey Street to get her some kosher wine for Passover—impatiently waits for the elevator to come up, and sometimes on Friday nights I can hear her agitatedly walking up and down the hall waiting for the elevator, to the point where I go and play elevator man for her so she can stop mumbling in Yiddish at the top of her lungs outside my apartment door already.

I open the elevator door for everybody, and then ask everyone's destinations, remembering that according to custom, I will not be explicitly *asked* to do any work for anyone else, and a neighbor's friend says: "He must think we're crazy" in that vexing way of talking about other people in the third person within direct earshot of them, and my neighbor asks: "Are you Jewish?" which I am forced to deny once again—all the while recalling Lenny Bruce's comment that *every* New Yorker is Jewish—as she continues: "We have this thing called

'Shabbes'—" as I interrupt: "I *know* from Shabbes," which I do. More ironic is the fact that when the boyfriend and I (gay) and our friends Judy and Sharon downstairs (also gay) and various other friends (also also gay) get invited by my friends Marjorie and Sy to dinner on Friday (or any given holiday event), the chances of a Queer Quorum at the Cohens are pretty high, so much so that we start referring to it as "gay Shabbes," with Marjorie asking me matter-of-factly while coming up in the elevator: "So, are you coming down for gay Shabbes?" to the consternation I imagine of a neighbor in the elevator with us who probably now sees new evidence pointing to the Jews and the gays *conspiring together* on some paranoid the-world-is-run-by-*Them* level. She smiles, as I obligingly hold the door open for them as they exit, engendering in me a new neurosis that everyone in my building refers to me not as "that nice boy from the seventh floor" but more likely as "that *Shabbes goy* from the seventh floor."

Living on the seventh floor means more often than not having run-of-the-mill stress-relieving elevator conversation with my neighbors on the way down or up as the case may be, with the older women in my building wanting to know if the mailman has been here or not, and the men usually having something to say about the weather, and the resident Marxist-slash-entrepreneur breaking into revolutionary discussions of Communist history past and present that don't really begin or end but seem to pick up from whatever we were discussing the last time we met and that usually end with a *"Vive la France!"* thrown in for the boyfriend's benefit. Last year a new lady moved in across from me and frankly she is no more or less strange than anyone else in this building, and so I am not in any way on guard while we uncomfortably do not say a word to each other in the elevator one otherwise nondescript day like any other, since she isn't talking about her three cats, or my dog, or any of the banter we usually share but instead chooses to break the silence with: "Did you hear me screaming the other day?" I measure my words carefully as I reply, since I can't very well say: "Yeah, I heard you but didn't do anything about it," à la Kitty Genovese. I say: "No," while wondering nonetheless if I am supposed to ask what was wrong, which I guess I want to know, but I can't quite figure out the manners protocol of exacting such information. She only confuses me by blurting out: "My friends got married the other day," rather non-sequitur-like. Following her train of thought has so tired me out that I can't bring myself to ask whether this and the screaming are somehow linked, and she leads me even farther afield with: "I had to buy them a present, so I bought them glow-in-the-dark underwear." At this point I'm leagues behind in terms of her thinking process, for which there should probably be a Latin phrase that means non sequitur in a huge-leap-in-train-of-thought way, as opposed to regular change-of-subject-wise, not to mention my disbelief that someone might purchase such a wedding gift in the first place, as she brings us round to the original point: "I wanted to check and see if it worked, so I put it on, and went into my closet and closed the door and got locked in!" I say to myself that it isn't really necessary to try on the underwear to test it, that putting it in a dark box or looking at it in a dark room would have been test enough, but furthermore, how gauche to present a friend a gift of underwear much less a gift of underwear that *you have already tried on before-hand*, but what I say is: "I was not aware that our closets had locks on them." I nonchalantly emphasize the banal aspects of apartment hardware in the hopes of bringing the conversation back into the realm of the probable, but she swerves us back toward the conversational cliff looming before us as she exclaims: "Well, this one got stuck! And I was screaming for two hours before the neighbors downstairs heard me and called the super, who called the police, who broke into my apartment and opened the door!" as we thankfully arrive at the first floor. She says goodbye and leaves me standing there, the image of New York's Finest and the building's maintenance staff and the downstairs neighbors opening her door and finding her standing there in glow-in-the-dark underwear now burned indelibly into my brain for the rest of the day, causing me to blush whenever I see her from then on, and leaving me much too embarrassed to ever find out whether in fact the underwear actually *worked*.

Coming Out

Dykes save cities.
—Graffito found on West 92nd Street

Coming out to my siblings was a relatively painless process of asking two of my brothers and my sister all on separate occasions whether "I need to explain about [the boyfriend] Hervé and me," with my other brother point-blank asking me one day, and so I assume that it is equally obvious to my parents that the man I've been living with for twelve years who comes home with me to celebrate Christmas with the family is perhaps something more than my *roommate*, with my assumption that my parents won't ask me first and the knowledge that I won't bring it up first creating much in the way of mutual denial that I figure is *just fine* on a diplomatic eggshell-walking level, until I receive my father's worried phone call about my cousin Danny, whom he saw recently at my cousin Bill's wedding. His storytelling goes on to expand on the wedding, short-shrifting my cousin Danny's updated life information: how he is living in Manhattan, and more specifically Barrow Street in the Village just off of Christopher Street, and how he is living with a *roommate*, and how his roommate is a *graphic designer*; I ignore my father's wedding chatter for trying to put two and two together concerning my cousin Danny, who last time I spoke to him was working in the construction trade and living in the Bronx. The situation deteriorates the next day when my sister calls laughing hysterically to explain that Dad thinks that since I am an *artist* I probably have a lot of *gay friends* and therefore should speak to my cousin Danny, whom my father is worried about and whom he *suspects may be gay*, and is further reduced to a complete debacle by my brother's call the day after that saying that he told Dad to "open his eyes" about the whole situation, the result being a long sustained silence for the rest of the car trip they were taking to my brother's graduation from Navy boot camp in Florida.

The benefit of the doubt that I give my father in terms of his knowing that I'm gay is upon reflection without any precedent in terms of us being on the same wave-length. During my sophomore year at Syracuse University, back in the days when the earlobe that a guy wore an earring in advertised his gayness (right) or straightness (left)—unlike today, when no part of the human anatomy is considered off-limits in terms of body piercing in some search for modern primitivism or primitive modernism as the case may be, and the unpierced peoples of the world have become strange out-of-place aberrations—my usually drunken-stupor self-inflicted style decisions imparted to me not only Great Street Cred but inflamed and infected earlobes as I tried to move as quickly as I could from the clunky women's stud earrings to actual much-cooler hoops, and usually through bad planning calendar-wise I would have to repierce everything later on as I removed the earrings before going home to my parents' house for vacation, not giving my poor perforated ears the slightest chance whatsoever to heal, convinced as I was of the coronaries my parents would suffer when their eldest son showed up wearing more ear jewelry than the female members of the family all put together.

My parents come to gather me and my things from school, and I greet them earring-less (although it seems to me that it was still pretty obvious since even today when I don't wear earrings anymore in an anti-piercedness-overboard-reaction kind of way you can still see my six piercings like strange fashion-based war wounds from long ago), and we all pile into the front seat with my stuff in the back, heading out for the long drive home and with me focusing unwaveringly on telling them that my ears are pierced, which, over the course of an eight-hour car trip, takes on huge out-of-proportion importance compared to all of the things I could possibly tell them about my life, especially the little secret tidbit about *being gay*, of course. We drive and drive as I begin to feel that pit-of-my-stomach churning feeling, not aided by my father's New-Yorker-out-of-New-York compulsive push-the-gas-pedal-to-the-floor driving style; I work myself into a state and, realizing that "earrings" and the discussion thereof are not going to simply pop up in conversation, I decide to just blurt it out but feel the need to get their undivided attention, so I call out: "Mom? Dad?" to the two people sitting next to me in the cramped car who are quite obviously my mother and father.

My father interrupts his nonstop commentary on other drivers' non–driving ability, which I am convinced is going to get him shot one day, especially since he New Yorker–like drives with one foot on the brake and one foot on the gas, which allows him to tailgate people while tap-tapping their bumper to remind them of how slow they are going; the car is quiet as my father has stopped mouthing off about the other drivers (who all seem to be named "Charlie") and pointing out the blinds of trees where he imagines the Pennsylvania State Police lie in wait for him personally as he slows down and speeds up accordingly; this is my cue to let go with my Piercing Announcement as I state as matter-of-factly as I can: "I have something to tell you." What happens next is rather blurred in my memory, as most white-tunnel-of-light occurrences probably should be: my father braces himself against the steering wheel, slams on the brakes without warning, and pulls over to the side of the road; my mother and I are convinced that we missed a car or an animal or otherwise avoided an accident but there is no one and nothing else around; my mother wants to know if my father is all right, and I want to know what is going on, and my father only manages to barely and gravely say: *"What."* I look at him, and I look at my mother, and I realize that there was no avoided collision, that my father's reaction is to *my statement* of having something to tell them. I try to backpedal a bit to the soften-the-blow preannouncement I should have started with, instead of thinking I could just up and out with it; I look at my father, still steeled against the steering wheel, and I say: "Well, I don't know if you noticed, but I kind of . . . well, I don't know if you saw my ears—" as my mother starts to laugh, saying, "Oh Dan, I noticed right away!" and my father closes his eyes, relaxes his arms, and finally exhales; I look at him and manage to say: "I got my ears pierced! What did you *think* I was going to say?" My father waits about two minutes to compose himself, and finally replies: "I thought you were going to tell us that you got some girl at school *knocked up!*" Comparatively speaking, this is such a much-bigger deal that my father doesn't react to the ear piercing at all, while I think to myself that my getting some girl *pregnant* is absolutely the *least* of his worries, but leave that little can of worms for another time when the man isn't behind the *wheel of a speeding automobile*.

The day after the phone call about Danny, my father informs me that he is "coming into the city"—which I remind him he hates to do ever since he left the city to move to New Jersey decades ago, the city during the Depression and World War II somehow remembered as being a better place than the city I now live in—with his need to talk about my cousin his justification, leaving me to worry endlessly as I pace up and down the hall looking at our one bedroom, and our one bed, and our one everything else, with the denouement suddenly arriving at dinner after much small talk when I finally blurt out: "I guess this is the point where either you ask me, or I tell you" to which my father responds: "Are you?" to which I respond: "Yes" to which he responds: "Okay."

The weight of years and years of worry and anxiety are lifted from my shoulders when my father simply states "okay" with no hitches or catches or attached riders; only now as the years have gone by it's gone to the other extreme, my father charging forward with the gay

liberation standard raised much higher than I might otherwise believe him capable of, subscribing to conservative publications and listening to conservative radio as
he does while antipodally looking to pick fights with
people as he outs me indiscriminately right and left,
or using us as an example of a stable relationship, or
defending the right of a gay couple—whom he refers to
as "the boys up the street" even though they are closer
to his age than to mine—to live undisturbed in their
prize-azalea-surrounded house in their suburban neighborhood in my rather-Republican hometown, which has
somehow managed to sprout a gay nightclub where the
bowling alley used to be right next door to the volunteer
fire department. My father's biggest worry in this regard
is that my aunt and uncle are not being supportive of my
cousin, or, worse, don't acknowledge it or admit it to
themselves, with my father figuring that it would be
better to just add his sister to the list of people he hap-
hazardly outs me to so that she would not feel "alone," or
without support, or anything else; and he calls her up
and tries to be consoling and comforting as he informs
her: "You know, Peg, our sons have something else in

common other than their first names..." and my aunt, not one to be nonplussed or one-upped by her younger brother, pauses a bit, and then, as only a deadpan New Yorker can, simply replies: "Well, Jim, we knew, the minute your Danny moved in with that *French hairdresser!*"

The Job

I want you to find me a chair, like an antique chair, but not too antique, and it has to be, you know, like those antique chairs that are painted and painted over so that the colors underneath, like, show through; and this is for the window display, so it has to be perfect—no damage—and the colors of the chair have to match our new line's colors EXACTLY.

—Overheard Gap employee

Reading the *New York Times* classified section want ads under the heading "College Grads" is a bizarre exercise in discovery in terms of how New York is seen through the eyes of would-be city dwellers eager for that First Job. The ads drip with one-step-removed allusions to media, fashion, and rock and roll in inverse proportion to the level at which the job of accountant or personal assistant or financial analyst is thought about in such terms. When I think about media and jobs I think about my friend Shannon, who worked at *The Financial Times* as a receptionist, pushing phone buttons and saying "Financial Times" fifty million times a day and realizing she has to quit when I meet her after work one day and she hits the elevator button and blurts out: "Financial Times!" When I think about fashion and jobs in New York I think about my friend Robby's sister Robin, who used to work in the Alaïa boutique downtown, where my friend Barbara and I sometimes would hang out just to watch in disbelief as people spend vast amounts of money on very tiny pieces of Lycra clothing, and some wafer-thin waif-esque Paulina-looking model comes up to us and just starts talking: "I was here a while ago? And there was a piece of Lycra that I liked? And it was black? And I don't see it now? And do you still have it?" proving what you've always known to be true, that models should not only not be seen but not heard as well, unlike what everyone at that abomination of a so-called entertainment cable channel thinks, and Barbara just keeps nodding her head until the Paulina-looking model finishes, at which point Barbara says: "Honey, we don't work here," causing the Paulina-lookalike to drop her Marlboros all over the floor. When I think about rock and roll and jobs I think about the Viacom building on Broadway, where a friend of mine works as an editor and where two other cable abomination so-called music channels are head-quartered and where twenty-something Golden Demographic Children work in their television studio that uses Times Square as a soundstage, causing great stress to people trying to walk to their *real* jobs, the only seeming required qualification for employment there being a birth date post-1972 along with an ability to wear co-opted-rebellion-esque klonky boots and black eyeliner and dyed hair in total denial of the fact that they work for a huge corporation that revels in the production of pure unadulterated *mediocrity*.

Many of those beginning jobs are described in bottom-of-the-barrel analogies of paying dues, or working one's way up the ladder, or entry-level ground-floor opportunity, when in reality climbing out of the bottom of a sand pit might be a better way to describe these first jobs-to-nowhere, like the post-Strand temp work I find doing word processing for the various firms in the marble-and-glass-buildinged financial district, at an investment firm where the head of personnel's office is twice as big as my apartment and my Faux Pas in neglecting to wear a tie requires a dozen phone calls to see whether I can obtain permission to go up to the executive floor, and then at an insurance company where entire substaffs of people do nothing but type up mind-numbing lines-of-numbers ledger sheets, and then at a financial firm where I am required to lie in French to some executive's mother that her son is not in fact in his office reading the newspaper with his feet up on his desk; in these jobs my usual pas-times include trying not to hang up on people when I can't figure out how to transfer calls, and figuring out where exactly my worked-on-in-stolen-time résumé is printing out, and counting the number of non–Good Ol' Boys inhabiting the outer executive offices, always finding that the glass ceiling is—worry not, O Captains of Industry—still Firmly in Place.

I find a job working a bizarre reverse-commute grave-yard shift from midnight to eight in the morning cobbling together existential bank consulting firm reports that recommend charging profit-inflating bank fees at the expense of scraping-by customers like me who get painted wooden ducks from the firm's president's trip to China at Christmas instead of bonuses that might put our bank accounts into that no-fee stratosphere that the consultants themselves enjoy, and although being alone all night with the desktop publishing computers and the copier machine results in the launch and a mini–print run of fifty copies of my zine, my contrary-to-circadian-rhythm lifestyle of working the night shift—coming home and making breakfast for Hervé then on his way to work, going to sleep, waking up and making dinner for

Hervé and me before heading off to work again—leaves me about one hour in the day when I actually see the person I'm ostensibly living with.

I find freelance work at home on a promotional magazine prototype for a major magazine publisher, which includes articles from many of that publishing house's stable of magazines that drive home the point that a lot of junk gets published on high-end glossy paper in full color by this one publisher only you wouldn't know it unless you were to see all of the magazines together at one time. One of my jobs entails having the covers of the magazines scanned in at some fly-by-night computer service place populated by people who all claim to be partners: "Let me pass you to my partner, Jim" they all seem to say, like a warped Marxist nightmare where there is no working class, only management; and working out of my apartment fills me with Great Ennui, as when I find myself typing up a sales manual for a major cosmetics firm including all of the new-makeup-line color names, such as "Fawn," and "Dusk," and "Rust," and "Moss," and "Fern," which reflect the springtime sensibility as described in the manual for the coming line in that weird trend-du-jour way the fashion and beauty industry have of endlessly perpetuating themselves, as well as being in stark contrast to the CNN coverage of the bombing of Iraq blaring from my television in the background, and all I can think is that it must be a lot more fun to work in the CNN design office doing up those snazzy typographic treatments reading WAR IN THE GULF in big orange fireball letters that outdo graphically the actual footage of Peter Arnett hunkered down by his umbrella-looking satellite dish beaming himself directly from the war scene, and that make me question the hold people in the media industry have on reality. Since we don't have a doorman, I basically have to stay inside the whole day when expecting messengers, who take their sweet time making their way uptown; one rather memorable messenger buzzes for about two hundred seconds longer than is absolutely necessary and then screams: "MESSEN-GEEEEEEERRRRRRRRR," as I can hear from the intercom long after I've buzzed him into the lobby, and then screams incoherent nonsensical babble that gets louder as the elevator approaches my floor, as I start to dread the elevator doors *opening at all*, which unfortunately ruins my usual bored housebound fantasy of buff biker boyz knocking at my door in a strange

The Postman Always Rings Twice sordid escape into celluloid-based reveries.

I spend a few more years working on various cup-of-angst-runneth-over projects, such as a how-to book on stained glass, and that magazine that catalogs women's distress during pregnancy and childbirth, convincing me that if God exists he's definitely *a man*, and a two-days-straight nonstop effort to do a saving-grace redesign of a home design magazine that finds me on the verge of an exhaustion-induced coma, only to be berated by the Jamaican cab driver on the way home for "working your bloody fingers to the bone for no pay to give taxes to *The Man!*" I work for a start-up magazine publisher doing business out of the Gumby-shaped Citicorp tower, whose architectural features include a big rock in an oil bath at the top to keep it from swaying and a slanted-for-solar-power roof off just enough degrees to make electricity generation impossible and a reinforced-in-the-nick-of-time internal skeleton structure and a glass outer surface that in particularly wintry conditions collects huge sheets of frozen precipitation that then plummet to the sidewalks twenty stories down like *Omen*-esque panes of decapitating glass which I watch fall to the cordoned-off sidewalk below when I am not watching the reflection of the reception area in the office window that is the wall in front of me to see who is hanging out in the office, especially when it's a certain not-known-for-editing editor stopping by while shopping around his political magazine-to-be who sits in the lobby unaware of my covert dreamy-eyed surveillance.

There's some slight irony to be found in a magazine publishing industry where most every publication is staffed by people who spend vast amounts of their lives working on huge treatises and articles and front-of-the-book sections on topics that they themselves have no connection to other than the twelve hours a day they spend at work, like the staffs of home decoration magazines who describe apartments that they themselves don't live in, or the staffs of garden magazines who talk about leisure time and landscapes that they themselves don't have or work on, or the staffs of sports magazines who summarize feats of athleticism that they themselves don't engage in, or the staffs of men's magazines who list the virtues of heterosexual mating patterns that they themselves aren't concerned with since they're *gay*, or the staffs of food magazines who introduce exotic locales from whence come exotic ingredients creating equally exotic dishes that they themselves never prepare since they *order out most every night*, yet on some level it is all quite appropriate since the readers of the same glossy four-color magazines don't usually *do* any of the things written about in the magazine *either*.

I work at a corporate-sponsored new media venture, with hundreds of employees corralled into cubicles like so much veal-to-be, separated from our parent company by a sword-of-Damocles thread—which makes pulling the plug that much easier when the venture eventually fails—and we have satellite dishes and news wires and television feeds and writers and editors and designers and programmers all working full tilt on a not-yet-launched Web site the number of viewers of which exactly equals the number of employees. Much of the day sees me patrolling the intercubicle pathways trying to find the person who thinks that a CD-ROM drive is an excuse to play Kenny G. at full volume; or the other person who speakerphones the livelong day not because she is busy doing something else but simply because she *can*, since when I tell her that I can hear her clear across the office instead of picking up the phone she basically just hunches closer to the speaker; when not in patrol mode I'm on the phone with my friend Juliann not two feet away in the cubicle right next to me, complaining about the cacophony of music coming from all directions, or the speakerphone girl, or asking her to tell me again the name of our CEO-du-jour.

The two floors below us are occupied by the triple whammy that is the New York offices of the Gap, Banana Republic, and Old Navy, decorated Ikea-style in faux plants in white faux-Grecian urns and a huge wall of televisions sets à la the Palladium (where I saw my first rock concert and depressingly enough soon to be an NYU dorm) and staffed by people who shop at the Gap during their lunch breaks and walk around in their brand-new Gap clothes and brand-new Gap back-packs and brand-new Gap accoutrements—which by themselves are already questionable to me in terms of ripped-off designs, and sweatshop fabrication, and no-relation-to-human-sizedness, and general one-wash-falling-apart-ness—and who go to Seattle on vacation because "Eddie Bauer is headquartered there"—which is a strange thing to know about a city—as overheard in the elevator where I dread anyone's pushing "4" or "5," and only made worse by the vacation-taker's response of: "I was going to work there, but I thought, I should come to New York, because, you know, if you want to work in fashion then you have to come to New York," which is interesting if only because it somehow equates Eddie Bauer and the Gap with fashion.

The eventual day comes when half of the entire company is called in for an early morning meeting and crammed into the news area—the other half being told not to come in until three P.M., evoking for certain employees of a certain religious belief a certain obvious analogy—only to be summarily dismissed by our CEO, who walks away vastly richer for the experience before going off to downsize some other company, and with workers in nether offices in Massachusetts having the distinct displeasure of being fired via *remote phone hookup*. The indignity of getting fired from the job I've just spent fifty-plus hours a week for ten months working at is only surpassed by having to carry the salvaged effects of my short corporate life down in the elevator accompanied by the Gap robotrons entering from their video-walled and fake-pine-tree-riddled reception area yammering on and complimenting each other: "Nice jacket, is that Gap?" yet *still employed*, as the officeful of people above gets its walking papers, crystalizing for me in one long cruel elevator-ride minute the notion of a sick, perverted, unjust world.

Why I Stay?

In light of the aggravation that is living in New York City, psychiatrists have become aware of a new classification of illness inherent to the East Coast, and more specifically, New York. Doctors are hard-pressed to name these new afflictions as quickly as they crop up:

YUPAGORAPHOBIA: Rational fear of Brooklyn Heights.

TUNNEL CARPOOL SYNDROME: Affliction of the hands caused by incessant horn honking coming into the city.

UMPTEENTH BAR SYNDROME: Depression caused by the realization that nightlife is next to nonexistent, only discovered after spending hundreds of dollars in one night looking for it.

My New York life has always been primarily one of small rituals and self-imposed neurotic rules; among these are certain rules involving not frequenting establishments that don't display a minimum of courtesy or manners on the phone or in person; and not going to bars that have televisions in them since I can *not* pay money and watch television *at home*; and favoring smaller local merchants where the prices might be a bit higher, but which make me feel slightly more anchored to my community, since I would rather pay a little bit extra to have someone remember who I am, say hello, say thank you, give me credit on the rare occasion I'm a bit short on cash, and otherwise provide the mom-and-pop rapport that in New York has been replaced by corporate facelessness, than pay less but have to deal with people who shove change in my hand and then scream "NEXT!" in my face. Problems arise, however, when my rituals and rules no longer apply because the Bigger Picture is changing on a macro level completely out of my control, and my list of rules becomes unwieldy and prevents me from actually going out and doing things, with the above-mentioned rules only overridden by the fact that food shopping is one of the things that I have to do in terms of my corporeal survival since I can't write off eating the way I've written off going out to clubs, or movies, or concerts, or restaurants, or—now that I think about it—just plain going *outside in general.*

Part of the problem is the actual process of growing up and older in the city, with what I remember of course being in sharp contrast to what I see and experience today, with the above-mentioned Rules of Living created based on some notion I have of the actually rather recent Good Old Days—like going out to nightclubs in the city was fun for me the last time at Danceteria or Pyramid in 1983, but today barely runs off of a post-Warholian afterglow with the current claims to fame today involving being a Club Kid, or getting free drinks at a club, or being seen with Leonardo DiCaprio at a club, or committing murder and cutting up the body and putting the pieces in a trunk and then dumping it in the East River which then for some unknown reason becomes an actual news story in *The Village Voice*; or going out to concerts in order to recapture some nostalgic moment from my postadolescent years, like the Clash concert I go to where I manage to stare down some neo-punk moshing and otherwise pogoing on my foot, or the Debbie Harry concert in a small hall reminiscent of Blondie's CBGB roots except half the people in this club aren't even listening but rudely chatting among themselves during the entire set, or the Siouxsie & the Banshees concert at Roseland, where I find myself seemingly transported to the set of an impromptu revival of *Rocky Horror*, or some gothic version of a Cuban debutante ball for all of the black clothes and lace and hairspray, all of which leaves me quite out of place among this second generation of Lollapaloozers, wondering what happened to the divas of my youth, and feeling very very very *old*.

I've stopped going to the movies, for which I have very strict rules of viewing that don't include listening to other people's videos-at-home-induced talking back to the screen for the entire length of the film, or their predicting aloud what's going to happen, or their critically discussing the movie at length afterward in terms of how it relates to them personally; someday I imagine I'll end up like Baby Jane Hudson, or Norma Desmond, miserably watching movies alone but at least in a *private screening room*. I'm not quite certain when this everyone-a-critic shift in the General Psyche took place, but it is epitomized for me by an exhibition of Impressionist paintings in Paris, where I was standing a bit mesmerized in front of a self-portrait done by Van Gogh when my Personal Moment with Art was ruined by the man next to me needing to prove some art-historical point to himself stating: "Now, I don't know who this is a picture of, but you can tell by how it is painted that the artist is *crazy*." I likewise cannot stand the banter overheard after a movie gets out where no one is able to simply just appreciate *to themselves* a moment of Great Understanding in thinking about a film without explaining it in ridiculous solipsistic terms as if the movie itself was produced, directed, and filmed entirely for them and their so-so-exciting lives.

The so-called higher orders of culture do not bring any respite either, witnessed by my experience watching *The*

Barber of Seville at the Metropolitan Opera where the woman in front of me sees nothing wrong with unrolling her triple-layer-cellophaned sandwich in the middle of the first act. The exhortation of the surrounding crowd for me to silence her noisy noshing is met by my paralyzed non-response as I flash back to a Shirley Bassey concert I attended with Hervé and our friend Anne where we find ourselves in the balcony with a group of women behind us who are having a preconcert discussion of whether "Goldfinger" will lead off the concert or not. The dimming lights bring dread instead of anticipation since there seems to be a lot riding on the wager behind us, and, as the all-too-familiar trumpet sounds off, the woman behind me screams: "I knew it! I told you! I knew it would be 'Goldfinger'! Didn't I tell you it would be 'Goldfinger'?!" The dirtiest look I can muster to give her brings on a chorus of: "What's his problem?" as the concert devolves into a ninety-minute cascade of crying, and singing, and remembering past concerts, and carrying on, with my request of: "Could you please not speak during the concert?" only causing a discussion of how rude I am, and how dare I, and who do I think I am *anyways*.

Things are not helped by Hervé's rather commanding request of: "WOULD YOU PLEASE SHUT UP!" which is mockingly met by only more shrieking, and more crying, and more moaning at every song, and obvious enjoyment of the fact that the three of us are not enjoying much of anything at this point, with the final straw arriving when the woman behind me hisses into my ear after the final curtain: "It's a shame that some people don't know how to enjoy themselves!" causing me to stand up, wheel around, and start screaming: "I paid to hear *Shirley Bassey* sing! I didn't pay to hear *you* sing!" There is an entire balconyful of people now staring at *me* and *my* outburst, knowing nothing of what we just endured for an hour and a half; and the woman immediately launches back my way: "You JACKASS!"

Hervé starts in with a French-accented not-quite-right English retort, which is met by the gleeful return volley: "Go back to where you came from!" which is certainly most endearing when coming from second-generation Americans.

"Why don't *you* go back to *Astoria*!" I say, for reasons that still escape me to this day.

"You JACKASS!" they all five yell at me in unison.

"You . . . PIGS!" I muster up from some unplumbed depth of my being, scaring myself in the process, as we start lobbing sundry barnyard animal epithets at them like a demonic See 'n Say toy, in a fight reminiscent more of a kindergarten playground than the balcony of New York's premier concert hall. Finally I am obliged to sit down, my knees buckling under me I'm so upset as I take my seat, shaking, with random outbursts of ever-fainter "Jackasses!" filtering up from the stairwell, as they make their way outside, and with the strains of "Goldfinger" *to this day* bringing on shamed memories of fighting with women my mother's age who probably found the altercation an *added bonus* to their little concert outing that evening, as I now imagine myself sometime in the not-so-distant future buying up huge blocks of theater tickets so as to have a buffoon-free buffer zone of at least ten rows clear all around me.

At times I find myself hard-pressed even to just walk around the city the way I used to enjoy, with the neighborhoods that used to be defined by their Specific Commodity, such as SoHo's art galleries, and Chinatown's kitchen supplies, and Canal Street's World War II detritus not-junk-to-me stores, giving way to neighborhoods defined by the national chains and designer flagship stores that now make SoHo, or Madison Avenue, or lower Broadway no different from shopping in the Mall of America, as I see it Neighborhoods to Avoid rather than actual destinations; and with neighborhood food stores formerly reflecting the soul of the resident Ethnic Enclave disappearing little by little as neighborhood lines fade and change, with certain places retaining faint cultural traces to serve as tourist destinations.

And whereas the history of New York is one of transformation based on immigrant communities that come and go—like the former Norwegian community in Bay Ridge, Brooklyn, that I visited to buy some Christmas specialties for my parents' friend Gladys whom we've always known as Aunt Glady who grew up there, only to find that the one store left that sold Norwegian delicacies had long since boarded up and closed down, leaving me in a panic until some kind soul at the Norwegian embassy told me about the Seamen's Church in midtown where I could go and buy Norwegian foodstuffs like lingonberry preserves and various varieties of tubed fish paste, which I did to the great amusement I imagine of the assembled Norwegians in the church's social hall— there is something simply wrong in the way communities and neighborhoods are not being displaced by incoming *groups of people* so much as by incoming *block-wide megastores*.

For some reason, however, neighborhoods retain cachet even though the reason for that cachet has long since disappeared, like SoHo, whose art galleries have all moved east, as I try to explain to one of the groups of visiting French boys who happen to stay with us, reflecting the rather European trait of arriving in a foreign country backpack in tow expecting to find lodging in friends' apartments for weeks at a time and making me wonder whether our apartment isn't written up in some European bed-and-breakfast guide, and who want to go to SoHo on a Sunday which is nothing if not a nightmare. I beg off, saying that I'm not feeling well, and leave them with Hervé and turn around to go home. A block or so toward the subway I realize, upon instinctively checking my pockets to see if my money is still there—a completely obsessive habit of mine that manifests itself most often when I am traveling and I continuously check my passport not only to see if it is still on my person but to see if it is *still my passport*, opening it up and looking at the picture inside in a strange exercise of existentially verifying *my own bureaucratic presence on this Earth*— and I indeed see that my money is still there, but that my keys are not.

Turning around, I vainly search for them in the milling crowds, performing a real-life *Where's Waldo?* exercise only with no assurance that Waldo is even in the tableau; I call my neighbors in the hopes of heading home instead of trying to look for Hervé and his friends, but everyone is out because it's such a sunny day, my only recourse being to try and intercept them on West Broadway in the heart of SoHo, which for some reason has become a major Mecca for Euro-types who, in their strange notion of Euro-fashion, spend a lot of Euro-cash on leather clothing that I can't in any way imagine to be comfortable in the middle of summer. I run into my friend James whom I've known since high school and whom I am really glad to see, first because I'm really glad to see him, but second because I'm glad to be talking to someone and not any longer seeming like a big loser with no life and nothing better to do than stand on the street corner watching all of the tourists not at all going into the nonexistent art galleries that no longer define SoHo but that SoHo is still known for; and James tells me a story about how he found three thousand dollars in the street in a paper bag, which he imagines to be drug money and which I remind him he's lucky he didn't get killed over as James describes how he and his boyfriend used the money to decorate their new apartment, and I think to myself that he was really lucky to find three thousand dollars in the street but at the same time how typical it is that fate saw fit to reward someone else with an instant nest egg of three thousand dollars; meanwhile I'm stuck spending my Sunday standing in the one place that I could not possibly hate more to be standing in on a Sunday afternoon.

The other major neighborhood change is of course Times Square, which is now Disneyfied and otherwise cleaned up both literally and figuratively, leading me to imagine New Yorkers committing petty crimes and other sundry misdemeanors in order to bring back New York's good old *bad reputation* if only to clear the sidewalks of 42nd Street and Broadway awash in tourists and huge throngs of muddled masses who no longer visit

Chinatown, and Little Italy, and Harlem, and the Village with its age-old houses nestled along mews-like cobblestone roads, and Chelsea with its landmark cast-iron architecture of the Women's Mile, and every other part of the city reflecting its actual *history* and *culture* and *diversity*, but rather the Disney Store, and the Warner Brothers Studio Stores, and the Coca-Cola Store, and Niketown, with its huge workforce of clothes-folders yet in some strange pinnacle of an adman's wet dream with no actual stock of merchandise to sell, and pictures of multimillion-dollar-earning superstars on the walls as opposed to the throngs of factory workers earning thrice-nothing, and dimmed lights that force people to watch the three-story commercial showing in the atrium *of the very store that the commercial is for*; with 57th Street now Tourist Central bordering on a minor equivalent of Las Vegas and that city's strange status as a theme town where everything is a gimmick, where everything is cleaned of its rough edges, with absolutely no regard to historical veracity or context, and now featuring a "New York, New York" casino where the skyscrapers are all the exact same size and which I overheard a bus driver in Las Vegas say was designed to be: "really real." In a similar vein are the New York restaurant destinations that are no longer the local eatery featuring Chilean empanadas or the Dominican place that sells amazing café con leche or the truly Chinese-food-serving Chinese restaurant downtown but rather restaurants reflective of the new American need to be entertained simulacrum-style while dining, like that so-called restaurant with its haunted house theme, and that so-called café with its fashion theme, and that other so-called café with its rock and roll theme, representative again of a Las Vegas mind-set that has not only theme restaurants constantly outdoing each other in terms of pyrotechnics and special effects but also otherwise "normal" restaurants that now feel the need to provide this same sense of entertain-ment, witnessed while dining in a desperately-searched-for "fancy" restaurant near the Riviera casino in Las Vegas by the arrival on our table of "smoking bonbons" which consisted of a plate of dry ice and plastic-buccaneer-sword-skewered chocolate-covered mint ice-cream balls which—with the addition of a little water—resulted in a truly spellbinding fogbound dessert extravaganza that lasted all of three minutes while we sat there horrified, with our hands covering our faces unable on any level to process what was going on; as well as every other restaurant that drives out original New York ethnic eateries and replaces them with sterilized close-enough copies thereof which in Las Vegas are then given stereotypical names such as "Chan's" and "Ching's" or "Ah, So." My biggest fear is that New York will follow in the footsteps of Las Vegas, which—unlike everywhere else in the world, where original objects retain value based on their authenticity—is based on the premise of value derived from approximation and facsimile, as seen in the huge not-even-marble "David" replica in Caesar's Palace being photographed by people perhaps unaware of the original statue, or even the female stars at La Cage that everyone cheers for who not only are not the actual female stars but who *aren't even female to begin with*.

This focus on world's-a-stage life-through-entertainment living slowly encroaches upon a previously immune New York City, now best expressed in New York City taxicabs, where formerly the recorded voices of "typical" New Yorkers reminded you to take your belongings and ask for a receipt, a device that was amusing for a while, since they used voices from different people from different parts of the city, and I always seemed to manage to get the Jewish mother voice telling me not to forget to take my "personal belong-gings," but that for some reason they decided to change, so that now taxi riders are accosted by "famous" New Yorkers, who inflict their annoying schtick on other New Yorkers who don't care about their so-called celebrity status in the first place; if any place in the world seemed exempt from all-enveloping worldwide celebrity worship it was New York up until now, when the needling voices of Joe Torre, and Jackie Mason, and Judd Hirsch, and Joan Rivers, and especially Eartha Kitt and her cat-purr line delivery now make me willing to pay *double* the fare just so long as I don't have to be reminded by Catwoman *to take my stuff out of the cab.*

I retreat to my neighborhood, itself suddenly overrun with people walking around in brand-new faux-leather coats and brand-new clothes and brand-new shoes and driving around in brand-new unnecessary-for-city-driving four-wheel-drive vehicles, reading new magazines that expressly cater to the New Consumerists who wish to live in Manhattan because they see the *city itself* as a character from *Seinfeld* or *Friends*, like the Columbia University students I overhear on the train in their brand-new clothes that cost as much as their tuition talking about the places they've visited in the city so far which include the *Seinfeld* diner, and the *Seinfeld* soup-Nazi kitchen, and *Seinfeld*'s neighborhood, which I wish to remind them are all shot on a *fake soundstage in Los Angeles*.

These new city residents prefer the prelaundered sterilized mall environment of the new New York to anything "urban" or "hip" all the while wearing the trappings of "urban hipness" and "rebellion" in big klonky boots and leather jackets, and refried Beat khakis and turtlenecks sold to them (minus the messy political baggage) along with a bill of goods that they've also bought *individual expression* at the same time by the Gap, and Banana Republic, and every other national chain that takes *from* the neighborhood, and *from* the community, and *out of* the city while not putting anything back; these nouveau Banana Republicans are the selfsame people who don't mind the disappearing realness and encroaching fauxness likely to result soon in "New York–style" restaurants opening up *in New York itself*, with huge marketing campaigns surrounding the "new" and newly rediscovered New York–style salt bagels, and New York–style egg creams, and New York–style malteds, and olde-tyme New York–style barrel-gathered kosher dill pickles, and, I promise you, the relaunch of exorbitantly priced siphon-bottled faux-antique seltzer water.

I retreat to my apartment and look out my bedroom window, where the tippy-top of the Empire State Building that we formerly were able to see was jokingly referred to as our spectacular city skyline view but is now blocked by a huge so-called luxury apartment building rising on Amsterdam Avenue that someone found necessary to market with a slogan about getting something along the lines of "Two Parks for the Price of One," as if the parks are somehow a commodity that *belongs* to those paying high rents, oddly slighting the Upper West Side in its forced finding of something good to say about the neighborhood, going up as it is between two housing projects, across the street from the neighborhood bodegas and botanicas, on the site of what was once a community garden, which all in all is representative of *something*, though I'm rather afraid to actually admit to myself *what*, and I sometimes think that the suburbs I escaped long ago are now themselves moving into the city; that similar to my father I remember a New York that was but is no more; that like my mother, reminiscing about her daily bus trip to work up Madison Avenue when my parents first got married and lived in the city as we take a cab ride uptown and she tries to find something familiar among the plethora of designer shops now lining the sides of the street but is only able to recall the names of the ever-the-same churches, that my city too is gone; that history is revealed in pendulum swings often lasting longer than our very lives, with me riding this particular one in the wrong direction, all the while knowing in the back of my consciousness that just maybe this faux-facade of the new New York will be no match for the ivy-like tentacular resurging nature of the city's roots as newly resident city dwellers pick up the cycle in *their* newfound glowing-in-the-distance glorious city, full of life, full of possibilities, alive to a new irrepressible rhythm, and new stories waiting to be told.

About the Author

Daniel Drennan's work has been excerpted in *Harper's*, and he has appeared on the radio show "This American Life," produced by WBEZ in Chicago. He has written for *Print* magazine and the *AIGA Journal of Graphic Design*; he also publishes a zine, *Inquisitor*. He is coauthor of *The Digital Designer: The Graphic Artist's Guide to the New Media*. He currently lives in New York City.